HOME TO STAY

BECKE TURNER

SUNBERRY, NORTH CAROLINA

A place to call home.

Welcome to fictitious Sunberry, North Carolina. Settle back, put your feet up and prepare to enjoy a basketful of southern hospitality. With a population of twenty thousand diverse residents, Sunberry is the small city Americans dream of calling home. This slice of southern comfort offers a four-year college, an historic opera house complete with second-level entertainment, and a full-service hospital. No need to feel like a stranger. Sunberry residents mingle with new inhabitants, especially service members returning to civilian life.

If you're a veteran from nearby Camp Lejeune, a local rancher breeding organic cattle along the river, or a dog trainer developing new puppies to assist the disabled, you're bound to find a happily ever after in Sunberry. After all, doesn't everyone crave a home?

CHAPTER ONE

6:30 P.M.

Her boys couldn't be missing. Not today. Ava Robey checked the lane leading from Sunberry Road to the house. They weren't missing. They were late. And she had good news. They'd made it to the final round in the lease competition. If they won, Robey's Rewards would open in the only available commercial site on Main Street. One month of after-school and weekend work separated them from opening their new business.

But where were they? Her hand shook so hard she made the cut too short. One six-inch piece of trim and the laminate floor she'd installed would be complete. Her eyes moistened.

Breathe. Don't panic. They'll be here.

Hope, her five-year-old daughter, stepped over the toolbox and stood with her chubby hands fisted on her hips. "Where are my boys? The barn light is on."

Ava shoved an errant tendril into the Marine bandana tied around her head. "They're with a new friend. They'll be here soon."

Careful to keep her trembling fingers away from the saw's

edge, she cut another trim piece. Most days the wood scent, the smooth texture of the surface, and the dramatic transition of the project relaxed her. Not today. The pungent odor of the construction adhesive blasted through her sinuses like a lethal toxin.

Hope waited by her side until the scream of the saw died. "I don't like Kyle's friends."

"That's why we moved to Gran's farm," Ava answered, careful to hide the tension from her tone. "Kyle is making nice friends, now." She hoped.

Once she'd installed the final piece, Ava loaded her tools into Grandpa's hand-made box, wishing for his assurance that everything would work okay. So, what was keeping her three sons? They knew today was special.

6:35 P.M.

Ava straightened with a hand to her back, ignoring the aches brought on by hours on her hands and knees. Outside the front window, the leaves stirred along the desolate lane. She swallowed past a thickening in her throat. They're okay. Any minute, Kyle, Whit, and Nate would burst through the door with a hare-brained reason for their delay and hungry for dinner.

"We need to go get them," Hope demanded, her high voice indicating near melt-down mode. "They're going to miss Daddy's memory party."

"No, munchkin." Ava bent on one achy knee. "They won't miss it. They'll be here soon. Why don't you throw the ball for Toby?"

The black lab sleeping near the pantry lifted his head and drummed his broad tail against the new wood floor.

Hope stomped a booted foot. "I want to eat!"

"I'll make dinner in a little while."

"Two minutes?" Hope held up two stubby fingers.

Breathe. It's not her fault the boys are late. "In ten minutes you can help me set the table for the party."

Hope brightened and raced to the throw pillow in front of the TV screen. "Jiffy is ready for my memory." She held up the battered stuffed pig. "See? I gave him a bath last night so he'd be pretty and clean."

"Good job."

Before her daughter noticed her tears, she picked up the toolbox and exited through the back door, the hinges creaking from her hasty retreat. Keeping her back to the doorway, Ava deposited the toolbox along the wall, pulled a wadded tissue from her pocket, and blotted her eyes. The last shards of daylight dropped behind the trees and darkened the orange and yellow leaves. Twilight blanketed the old farmhouse like depression had blanketed her life five years ago. She'd survived those dark years, like she'd survive her boys' teen years. Because after tonight, they'd be grounded until graduation!

"You need to call my boys and tell them to come home right now." Hope said, startling Ava with her proximity. "I see stars."

Ava shuddered. Why had she taken Kyle's cell phone? Because he'd left her no choice. And why hadn't she questioned him about the new friend when he'd called for permission? He had a new friend, and he'd called to ask. She'd been thrilled by his consideration. Two hours ago.

Keeping her head turned from the intense scrutiny of her daughter, she opened the cupboard door, and removed six plates. How did she fix this? She couldn't call the friend, couldn't drive to the house. She couldn't even call the police. What would she say? My boys are late for dinner? What if they'd been abducted?

Don't panic. They weren't little kids. All three had topped her five feet seven inches over a year ago. Sunberry, a small city located near the North Carolina coast, had its share of small-time crime. But who would pick up three boys? Not one lone child, who could be overcome and intimidated, but three good-sized adolescents who had seen the better side of far too many disagreements.

The dishes clattered in her trembling fingers. Had Kyle found trouble in Sunberry already? She'd hoped he would grow out of his rebellious streak, focus on his schoolwork. He was smart—and angry. Had he done something bad? Led his two younger brothers into trouble? A memory of Kyle's dark eyes once bright and loving faded into his current dark-edged gaze.

Hope tilted her head to the side. "Are you going to cry?"

Ava closed her eyes, inhaled, and then blew out a breath. "Not if I can get a hug from you."

Plump arms encircled her neck. She couldn't lose Hope or her boys. Ava hugged Hope close to her chest, careful to avoid squeezing too hard.

"Ooo," Hope cooed.

Heavens, she loved that funny sound, the tickle of her daughter's silky curls, and the scent of her strawberry shampoo. But her heart continued to race.

6:50 P.M.

Headlights illuminated the lane and Ava shifted for a better view through the front window. Her heart pounded *lub-dub, lub-dub* in her ears. The boys had ridden their bikes to school this morning. A big black SUV bumped through the lane ruts, bouncing the beam of light across the living room wall. Thank goodness, it wasn't a police car. Although all traces of saliva abandoned her mouth, she swallowed past the constriction in her throat. *Never show weakness.*

The SUV stopped in the drive behind her aging Ford Explorer. When the headlights blinked out, the outlines of multiple passengers moved beneath the interior light.

However, the tinted glass obscured the occupants' identities. The driver's door opened and a large man, dressed in desert fatigues, straightened in the dim light from the porch.

A memory sent a chill racing along her spine. The set of his wide shoulders seemed familiar. When he looked up, her heart skydived to the pit of her stomach and she slapped her palm over her mouth. No! Not now, after so long. Captain Murphy, a man she thought she'd never see again, moved toward the back of the SUV. Her three missing sons trailed behind him.

"Why you?" she whispered.

While Toby whined from his position at the front door, Captain Murphy helped lift the boys' bikes from the cargo area of the SUV.

Hope stepped beside her. "Are my boys with a stranger?"

Ava gripped the window ledge. How did she explain to her children the man in her driveway had given their father his final, fatal orders?

When she jerked on the doorknob, the door scraped against the threshold announcing yet another item on the repair list for Gran's old house. Now her sons had joined that list. Looking guilty as sin, they stood behind the Captain, their gazes fixed on the weathered porch boards.

From the other side of the screen, the Marine stared at her. "Ms. Robey."

Ava stepped back. "Come in. From the looks of the boys, your story will require time and a meal."

Fifteen-year-old Kyle shot her an uneasy glance but moved forward.

Whit, her second son, followed, his bright blues moist with unshed tears, a gash bisecting his right brow. "Sorry, Mom."

She reached to inspect his face. "Are you okay?"

He ducked out of her grasp. "It's nothing."

Ava lowered her hand. This wasn't the first time one of her boys had suffered a cut or had come home late. But they'd never done it on November third.

With the tattered pig clutched under her arm, Hope gave her three brothers a fierce look. "You made me wait for Memory Night. I'm not coloring any more pictures for you!"

"Shh, honey." Ava moved Hope aside to let them enter. "Let Mommy handle this, okay?"

"I've been waiting forever." Hope's pouty bottom lip trembled.

"Thank you for your patience. Now, go feed Toby so I can talk to this gentleman." Ava gave her sons a no-nonsense look to let them know they were in deep trouble. "We'll talk later. Clean up for dinner."

She met Kyle's angry brown eyes, so like his father's. For a moment, her resolve wobbled. Near the cusp of manhood, Kyle tested her authority at every opportunity. She squinted. Was his jaw swollen? When he glared back at her, she pointed toward the hallway. "Ten minutes and we're sitting down for dinner."

With her breath held, she waited. *Come on, Kyle. Don't display the family wrinkles in front of the Captain, even if we aren't military anymore.*

Fourteen-year-old Whit, the family peacemaker, wrapped one arm around Kyle and the other around twelve-year old Nate. Together, the boys started down the hall, two dark heads surrounding her fair-haired middle son. After two steps, Kyle looked over his shoulder, anger still glittering in his glance.

"He always has to get in the last word," she muttered.

"He's smart," Ryan spoke from behind her. "Men like Kyle make good Marines. *If* you can turn that anger into a constructive outlet."

She whirled to face him. "You can't have him. You can't have any of my sons."

Unlike Kyle, Ryan didn't break her gaze. Standing at well over six feet tall, he filled Gran's small entryway. Sorrow, not rage, however, glistened in his eyes. Compassionate eyes—the same as her second born.

Heat flashed up her neck and face. "Sorry, it's—" She motioned toward the adjacent kitchen. "Please, come in and sit down. Coffee?"

He pushed away from the doorjamb and followed her. "Don't go to any trouble on my account."

"You brought my sons home. Coffee is the least I can do." She placed two white mugs on the counter. "I hope decaf is okay. I avoid caffeine after noon."

She placed the coffee in front of him, noting the stiff set of his features. Ryan Murphy had a bigger than life presence, dwarfing her country-style kitchen. Even sitting at the long plank table built for a family of eight, his wide shoulders and long legs seemed too large for the bench her three sons usually occupied.

She glanced at him before removing the pitcher of batter from the refrigerator. "I've been laying new floor, so I mixed pancake batter before I started. Three growing boys are hard to fill. I always make a double recipe and have plenty."

He looked like he had a bad case of poison ivy and didn't know whether to scratch or suffer. At least that was her take. She'd never been able to read him. He'd been from a prominent Sunberry family. She'd grown up on the farm. Although her husband Josh had liked and respected Ryan, she'd only been around him in later years at functions like the Marine Corps Ball.

While he sipped coffee behind her, she prepped the grill and poured syrup in a saucepan to warm. After ten years as a military wife, the rules remained stamped in her brain. Josh was enlisted. Ryan was an officer. She'd never seen Captain Murphy attempt to link the gap. In all fairness, the military wives often bridged the ranks and Ryan was single. At least he used to be.

When she sat at the table, he straightened. "So, you installed the floor by yourself?"

"The boys help me on the weekends. I finished the living room about ten minutes before you arrived." A burst of pride flamed in her chest. She'd done a good job once she'd figured out how to cut the corners.

"A woman with tools? I'm impressed. My sisters might have hung a few posters if I wasn't available." He smiled, and his features underwent a startling transition.

Her hand drifted to her chest. Amazing how a simple expression changed a man's looks.

She shrugged to hide her unexpected reaction. Must be the dimple on the right side of his mouth.

"Gran's house is rough. No one's lived here in years. When Mom and I opened the door that first day, we almost high-tailed it back to Charlotte."

"Sorry to hear about your mother."

Her breath hitched. Despite the leaking roof, deteriorating floors, and molding walls, she and Mom hadn't given up, hadn't given in to weakness. They'd laughed so hard they'd cried. Ava blinked. They'd had a good run. She wiped the tear at the corner of her eye and sipped her coffee, letting the warm liquid soothe her the same way Mom once had.

She blew out a breath. "So, what's the story on my boys?"

The man wasn't model material. His nose had a bump in the middle and his chin-line bore sporadic pock marks from teen acne. Still, he had a confident look—like a man who knew and understood himself and his world. A jab of resentment poked at the back of her mind. He hadn't known too much about Afghanistan. Otherwise Josh would still be alive.

"They were in a fight. I broke it up. Afterward, I made a deal with them. Based on your approval, of course."

The thought of being obligated to the man caused her fingers to curl around her mug. "Captain Murphy."

"Major now, but please, call me Ryan."

"Ryan." His name rolled off her tongue smooth as hot syrup on cakes. "Thanks for bringing my boys home. There's light traffic on our road, but I don't like them riding their bikes on it after dark."

He held up his palm. "I'd like to give your boys time to tell their side of the story before we talk. There's nothing worse than having a grown-up rat you out before you get a chance to come clean." He paused, opened and closed large calloused hands. "I mean if it's okay with you." He dipped his chin. "Sorry. I'm used to making decisions."

Big surprise, there. Still, she liked the idea. Not because it was his. Truth be known, she wanted *not* to like it.

"If there are any..." He held her gaze. "Holes in their account, I'll bring you up to speed afterwards. Since I'm involved, I've also got an idea about consequences—at least how I want to be repaid."

Repaid? Okay, she *really* didn't like that, especially when they were close to acquiring their dream. What the dickens had her boys gotten into? She sipped the decaf and released a slow breath. The time she'd charged into the principal's office to find her boys had told her *part* of the story flashed in her mind.

"Fair enough." She stood. "Boys! Five-minute warning."

When she topped off his cup, the steam swirled upward. "Family dinner time is important. That's when we talk. How many cakes do you eat?"

He pushed to his feet. "I'll come back after dinner."

"Don't." Blood pounded in her ears. "Dinner is my way of

thanking you for bringing them home. Don't take that away from me."

His gaze sparked with an emotion she couldn't read. "Three big ones or six small ones."

When she removed the griddle from the pan drawer, the metal clanked grating against her already frayed nerves. Darn her boys for putting her in this situation. She wanted them to like Sunberry, make friends, be normal. Heat flushed her cheeks. This better not be the new Robey normal.

Major Murphy remained ramrod straight, his sleeves rolled up his forearms, but his gaze flicked around the area. Josh used to do that. He never missed a thing. She sprayed the marred surface of the grill to keep the pancakes from sticking. Everything about the scene was flawed—like Gran's rundown place, her holey jeans, faded Marine t-shirt, and her hair tied beneath one of Josh's old handkerchiefs. At least the new floor looked good.

The gas burner on her range sputtered and then flickered to life along with something long buried within her—awareness of a man. Her scalp tingled, and guilt churned her stomach. She'd buried Josh five years ago and not one time had she thought of a man—any man. Right, like a widow with four children and a sick mother had time to think about a social life. Heck, she hadn't even seen an eligible man in the last year—unless she counted Bennie, the handy man she used for jobs exceeding her skills.

"Mom and I moved back to Sunberry because Kyle kept making the wrong kind of friends in Charlotte."

The batter hit the griddle with a sizzle, breaking the silence.

"Whit tries to talk Kyle out of getting in trouble. Nate doesn't challenge anyone. He follows his big brother." Stop babbling. The man didn't need to know about her family problems. But one thing he *did* need to know.

She turned to gauge his reaction. "Tonight is Memory Night."

Silence. Within seconds he stiffened with a slide of his boots and a widening of his eyes. Her breath hissed through her teeth. He knew the significance of the date.

"Every November third, we share a memory to remember and honor Josh." Her voice, rusty at the start, sounded stronger. "We'll all share a memory about Josh. You'll go last. I'm sure you can come up with something to tell them about their father. After that, the boys will explain why they were late."

When he started to push to his feet, her blood heated.

"Josh was a good man." She glared at Ryan. "You owe his sons at least one story about their dad."

CHAPTER TWO

TALK ABOUT A SHIT STORM. RYAN TENSED. TIME TO LOOK away, bolt for the door. He didn't move, didn't drop her hard stare. Didn't dare to. He'd faced down a lot of hostiles, but none with Ava Robey's intensity.

"Yes, ma'am. I can do that." He hoped his firm tone hid the yellow streak climbing up his spine.

She studied him like he'd become her latest target and then turned back to the range. He breathed. Next time he came across a teen fight, he'd keep on rolling. But what were the chances out of twenty thousand Sunberry residents he'd stop a fight with his Sergeant's kids? He gulped the coffee and burned a trail down his pipes. With that kind of luck, he should buy a lottery ticket.

No, he should've met his responsibilities. When he'd heard about Robey's death, he'd written a personal letter and asked to accompany the Casualty Assistance Calls Officer to notify her. But his responsibility to the family hadn't stopped. Mom told him Ava had moved to Sunberry. But he'd put off touching base with her, put off memories of the past. He owed Robey his life and now his widow— Ryan tracked her too slim frame while she prepared the meal. *Admit it, Marine.* The woman with tools had him wound tighter than a drill bit.

"I called after—" After what? Your husband was blown to bits? "after the funeral. I always got the answering machine or a kid. Probably Kyle. I left messages."

She didn't look away. But the pain in her golden eyes shone as sharp as the cramp in his gut. No more procrastination. He needed to help her out, ease the acid eating him from the inside out.

"That was a challenging time for me and my boys." The low timbre of her voice stripped the last scab protecting his conscience.

The urge to touch her and ease the memory curled his fingers into fists. "Yes, ma'am. That's why I called. I thought I could help. Take the boys to the movies. Fix your refrigerator. Whatever you needed."

She could mow down an entire unit with one of those looks. And he couldn't even defend himself because his tongue seemed to blow up in his mouth. The coffee might help, but his luck, he'd choke.

"I had a family to raise. I didn't need sympathy. I needed to pick up the pieces of my life and get on with it." She held his gaze again. "Do you understand?"

A raw edge still honed her glare, but the vulnerability he'd seen earlier had vanished. He'd known plenty of hard case Marines who had problems asking for help, namely his friend Schmidt. This was the first time he'd seen the same trait in a woman.

"A Marine is trained to take on whatever's thrown his way." He held her gaze but softened his tone. "But when he's down, he counts on his brothers to get him back on his feet. No man left behind. That's not just in theatre. It applies at home too."

His words curled his toes in his boots. *Way to go, Marine.*

She wasn't a private straight out of bootcamp. She was a woman still mourning her husband.

"Thank you," she murmured.

Swear to God, he felt like throwing himself on his sword. She stared and he stopped bobbing his head like one of those bubbleheaded toys. He hated when he did that. It usually happened when he was in a tight spot—which was coming too often around Ava Robey.

Her distant look would probably haunt his dreams. Feeling that deep came from secrets a person didn't want to share. He knew because he had a few secrets too. Combat did that to a man. Loss did that to a woman. Mom had shown the same signs after his dad died.

"Marines serve and protect." He scrambled for something, anything to assuage the pain in her eyes. "That applies to families. As Sergeant's wife, you and your family are part of the Marine family."

Just the thought of losing the support of his Marine family sent a shudder across his shoulders. He couldn't imagine a life without them. Yet Ava didn't seem to know a life with them. He'd have to fill that vacuum for her. It was the least he could do for Robey's widow.

The timer on the range chimed and the haunted look evaporated from her features. When she opened the oven door, the savory aroma of bacon filled the kitchen. His stomach grumbled.

"I'm sorry. I should've returned your calls." She switched off the oven but didn't turn to face him. "At first I didn't want reminders of Josh. It wasn't you or the Corps. I needed time."

"I'm still here." This time he wouldn't let her down.

She faced him. "We're doing fine."

"Yes, ma'am." But she wasn't. Her boys were fighting and the farm was crumbling around her ears. A way to sugarcoat the truth would be helpful, but none came to him.

"You said you left Charlotte because of the oldest. There are lots of Marine families with teenagers at Lejeune. I could hook you up with a few. You know, like a support group of mothers."

As if on cue, the two younger boys entered the kitchen. She narrowed her eyes on him but didn't say what she was thinking. Which was probably a good thing. He'd pushed too hard. But he was trying to help. She had her hands full. Even an old bachelor like him could figure out that one.

The two boys fell into a rhythm and Ryan guessed this was the Robey routine. He'd bet his sidearm tonight was a subdued version of a usual night in the household—especially with three adolescent boys. Boys? They could be a handful. He'd had his share of experience coaching sports teams for the base kids, not to mention troops fresh from boot camp.

Ava added pancakes to a stack on a serving plate. If he remembered right, her family originated in Sunberry and later moved to Charlotte. He'd first seen her again at the Marine Corps Ball. She'd seemed taller. Probably wore high heels. Her toes had peeked out beneath her gown. Funny, what a guy remembered. She'd worn bright pink polish to match her dress. Robey kept her close that night—loving and proprietary to assure every man understood the beauty on his arm belonged to him.

Kyle barged into the kitchen, his dark hair wet against his scalp and anger simmering in his gaze. Ryan sipped his coffee. The kid had grit. No rounded shoulders or tail-between-the legs for Robey's oldest. This one was all attitude. Ryan squared his shoulders. A hot-headed kid called for a smart man to be on the ready.

A cough broke the silence and Ryan turned toward the two younger boys. They exchanged a glance, a nonverbal messaging system. Kyle was testing boundaries and his brothers knew it. They also didn't like it. Ryan had figured

Kyle, the oldest and smartest, held the alpha position when he'd first come across the boys and the ... situation they'd created.

Ava placed a plate piled high with browned pancakes on the table and the doughy scent caused Ryan's stomach to rumble. The big lab, resting on the rug along the wall, whined and repositioned. Whit brought over a platter of crisp bacon and Nate poured warm syrup from the saucepan into a serving pitcher.

The girl hurried to the table with a ratty toy that looked like she'd pulled it out of the dog's box. She pointed a chubby finger at him. "You're sitting in Grandma's chair."

With a mother's gentle touch, Ava smoothed the girl's long dark curls. "Mr. Ryan is joining us for dinner."

Although the kid continued to watch him, she climbed into her seat. Ava handed the pancake platter to him with a stand-down look that sent his heart rate hauling butt in retreat. Which is what he wanted to do. And he thought he had the chops to stand up to any fight—until he met Ava Robey. He forked three cakes onto his plate and returned the plate to her. Her house. Her orders. He owed her that. Owed her husband more.

Her solemn gaze held his, never wavering. So, did she regret asking him to share a meal as much as he regretted accepting her invitation? Maybe guilt drove her the same way it hammered him. Maybe she tried to work through the wounds of the past the same as any Marine who had seen battle. The same as Schmidt, hiding symptoms of PTSD.

She served one cake for herself, slipped one onto her daughter's plate, and handed the platter to Kyle. "Share your story, please."

With a sullen glance at first his mother and then Ryan, Kyle extracted a rock from his pocket and placed it in front of his milk glass.

"Dad told me when he was deployed, I had to be the man of the house. No matter what, I had to hold up for my brothers. He didn't ruffle my hair or treat me like a baby. He made me look in his eyes and stand tall."

"Thank you, Kyle. Your father was proud of you." She gave the girl a reassuring smile. "All of you."

Ryan bit the inside of his mouth to keep his lips straight. This wasn't the time to smile or crack up. Ava would be all over him for encouraging her sons. He admired them. Based on the slight twitch of her mouth, she did too. Besides, the oldest boy gave an okay tribute.

She turned to the tow-headed kid. "Whit."

He placed a similar stone on the table. "One time when I was sick, Dad climbed into bed with me. He didn't worry that he'd catch something. He said a good man listens more than he talks. That made me feel good because I couldn't talk like the other kids."

Nate thumped his rock against the surface of the table. "Dad missed Father's Day at preschool because he was in Iraq. I hated it. My friends' dads came and talked about their jobs. My dad had a cool job and he wasn't there to tell my class, so I sat like a lump. When he got home, he came to my school. He showed his medals and talked about training. My class thought he was awesome. I'll never forget that day."

The girl shoved the tattered toy on the table, and Ava steadied Hope's milk glass to avoid a spill.

"Dude," Nate said. "Don't put that gross thing on the table."

"Mom!" Hope whined.

"It's fine, Hope," Ava soothed. "Tell us your story."

Ryan marveled at the girl's tiny hands stroking the raggedy toy's back. "I was iddy-biddy when my daddy was home. He bought me piggy and said he'd be back in a jiffy. So,

I named him Jiffy like Daddy told me. And I gave him a bath last night so he's not stinky like Nate."

Ryan covered a chuckle with a cough. Leave it to the cute girl to cause a revolt. While Ava calmed the war rumbling among the natives, he tried to frame a story suitable for Robey's kids.

Ava fingered the bare ring-finger of her left hand. "Your dad was always working to ensure everything around the house was in good working order before he deployed. He wanted us safe and cared for even when he couldn't be here."

And Ryan was supposed to pick up the slack. Although he'd kept track of her progress in Charlotte, the distance morphed into an excuse and only cowards hid behind excuses. Shame heated his face. He'd failed before, but he'd start to change that—as soon as he came up with a story to share. There'd been countless encounters. Sergeant Robey was his most trusted Marine. But that didn't mean he could share it with his family. Sweat beaded along his sides and the hard chair dug into his butt.

"Now for our guest." Ava seemed to stare right through him. "Mr. Ryan is a Marine. He was deployed with your father and agreed to tell a story about your dad."

Nothing like being in the crosshairs of five hostiles. The boys had no idea who he was when he broke up that fight. Now, they did.

He set down his mug. "Sergeant Robey was the best man in my unit. I depended on him for the hardest jobs and he always came through. Your dad was a hero. I owe my life to his quick actions."

"Like in the movies?" Nate asked, his eyes wide with wonder.

"Combat is not like the movies." The smell of enemy fire, the cries of wounded men, and the taste of fear bombarded him.

"Dad saved your life?" Whit asked, his steady blue gaze knifing Ryan's insides.

Ryan sipped his coffee, but the situation required a stronger drink.

"How?" Kyle said.

Ava's gaze darted to his. She would stop the questions. All he had to do was give her a sign. He shook his head.

"Our unit was ambushed. I got hit in the leg and went down. Your dad came back for me. He ordered me to *hold on* and his words got me through."

A black wall clock ticked in the silence. Ryan's right eye stung. When he wiped at it, sweat slicked his fingers.

"Thank you for sharing your story with us." Ava's quiet tone cut through the silence. "Josh was a good father and a good Marine. Be proud he was your father."

Ava pushed her plate forward. "Now that we've honored him, I think you should tell me why you were late tonight."

Ryan released a breath. He'd underestimated Robey's wife. She was no pushover. Her narrowed gaze roved from son to son like a drill instructor assessing new recruits. She checked the swelling around Kyle's left jaw, moved to Nate's split lip, and ended at the cut opening Whit's eyebrow. When she sipped her coffee, Ryan had to cover a smile with his napkin. The lady had timing down to a science. She'd raised her family alone for over five years. That couldn't be easy. And he'd neglected his duty to assist a fallen Marine's family. Time to remedy that oversight.

"It's my fault," Whit was saying. "Derrick made fun of Talley's braces."

Ryan wiped his mouth. Now, he was starting to get this picture. The bully who had started the drama and the stepson Schmidt had complained about were the same kid.

"Talley?" Ava said. "Is she the new friend?"

"Yeah, she's cool," Kyle said. "She helped Whit at school."

Whit poured syrup on his pancakes. "She's sensitive about her braces. Derrick was being a dick."

"Language," Ava reminded.

"Derrick Schmidt's a fathead. Big football star. He sucks." Whit stabbed at the pancake.

Ava wiped her mouth with her napkin. "Who threw the first punch?"

"Dad always told me to stand by my brothers." Kyle scraped off a small pile of bacon strips on his plate. "The asshole—"

"Language," Ava said.

"Whatever," Kyle said. "The bully called Whit a dimwit."

When Whit's face flamed with embarrassment, Ryan squeezed his fork. He hated a bully, especially one who preyed upon a trait that couldn't be helped. He'd noted the odd pattern of the kid's speech. The middle son must have a language issue. Except for his too-long blonde hair, the teen looked okay. His problem must be on the inside. Those always hurt the most.

"That's not nice," Hope said.

"Boys, we've had this discussion," Ava said. "Words don't start fights."

"He was asking for it." Kyle bit into a strip of bacon and moved it to the side of his mouth. "I told him to back off, but he kept coming. Big football dick going to show the poor kids how Sunberry High works."

"So, am I hearing that it was three against one?" Ava said.

"Try seven to four." Kyle's voice was more snarl than speech.

Ava's brow furrowed in confusion "When did this happen?"

"Right after school." Whit kept his eyes downcast. "Talley stayed to help me finish a homework assignment. That's when she asked us to come over for a while. We weren't bothering them."

"And no one at the school saw this?" Ava said.

"They stopped us at the corner."

"Derrick drives a cool SUV with dark windows." Nate spoke for the first time. "We didn't know half the team was inside."

Ava pressed her fingers against her forehead. "Go on."

Kyle's anger had diminished with the telling of the story. "Talley might've said something. They got out."

"I hit him." Whit's words came out in starts and stops. "Couldn't help it, Mom.... I didn't care about... what he called me. He made Talley cry."

She gave Whit a slight nod. "So the three of you took on these boys?"

"Talley got in a few good kicks. She has some ridiculous karate moves." Nate moved his hands above the table. "Can we take lessons?"

Ryan scraped at the syrup on his plate. If he didn't do something, he was going to start laughing. The Robey kids were too funny. No doubt, the household was utter chaos. Compared to their household, he led a boring, utilitarian existence. Maybe that's why they intrigued him.

"Right now, we need to get the story." She turned to Kyle with a stern look. "The *whole* story."

"After Whit hit Derrick, two of his friends jumped Whit from behind." Kyle chased down his food with a gulp of milk. "I was trying to break it up."

"Sure you were." A hint of sarcasm tinged Ava's words. She turned to Nate. "And you?"

"They were all over Whit and Kyle. I might have pushed one of the guy's head against the ground."

"We would've beat them if he hadn't come along and broke it up." Kyle nodded toward Ryan.

Ava raised her hand. "And that's all of it, the whole story?"

The boys exchanged glances and for a minute Ryan wondered if the trio would come clean.

"Talley was still pissed when we got to her house." Kyle turned away from Whit's glare.

"This wasn't the first time Derrick's made fun of her," Whit said.

"But this was the first time she'd had help," Ava guessed.

"Derrick kind of deserved it." Nate wrinkled his nose. "But his dad lost his mind when we hit his car."

Ava turned to Ryan with those big doe eyes and holy crap, his insides turned to mush. Now, he'd lost *his* mind.

She turned back to face the boys. "What did you hit the car with?"

"It was just tomatoes," Whit said.

Ava's chin dropped toward her chest and she mouthed the word *tomatoes*. That part had caught Ryan off-guard too. Kids usually threw rocks or sticks. But not this group.

"So you rescued them twice in one day?" she said.

"Colonel Schmidt lives behind me. There's common ground between us, but Schmidt sounds like a drill instructor when he's pissed." He shrugged. "I came out to see who was yelling."

"Thank you," she said.

The pancakes and coffee churned in his stomach. Sometime in the last twenty seconds she'd gone from ramrod stiff to soft and kissable. The woman was hot. A blind Marine could work that out, but that look. The gentleness in her hazel eyes and the hint of a smile on her lips generated something more than images of a few sweaty nights. A woman like Ava Robey made a man think about something with more substance.

But this wasn't the time to get involved with a woman,

especially one with four children. Fact was, he wanted to help Ava and her sons. But he'd also agreed to help Schmidt in some lease competition. And untreated PTSD was more serious than a scuffle among a group of hormonal boys. A Marine's life was on the line.

CHAPTER THREE

HER BOYS HAD DONE IT *THIS* TIME.

Ava resisted the urge to stomp her foot like Hope when she didn't get her way. Yes, she was proud they'd stood up to bullies. But starting a fight with seven older boys? Worse, her mom radar kept beeping her boys had omitted something. At this rate she'd have to delay the family goal, *again*.

"More coffee, Captain?" Thank goodness, her voice hadn't betrayed the bite of anger eating her insides.

He handed her his cup. "Ryan, please."

The way he'd drawn out the word *please* created a tickling in the back of her throat. It almost sounded...sensual.

"Ryan is easier." She hoped he hadn't noticed the slosh of coffee over the tops of their mugs. "Major Ryan is a mouthful. No wonder Marines use sir. It's like naming a dog Jeramiah or Ezekiel. Can you imagine hollering out the back door, 'here, Jeramiah?' By the time I said that, Toby would be a mile down the road."

The sound of his laugh urged her to move her feet like her favorite tune on the radio. It had been so long since she'd swayed to music. A longing for normal rushed through her. Ava blinked. She couldn't even define her normal.

"Let's take our coffee on the porch." Although an autumn breeze cooled the kitchen, Ava lifted the neck of her cotton t-shirt. "It's a beautiful evening." And she needed fresh air.

When the screen door slammed behind them, she released an unsteady breath. She'd never been a greedy woman. But tonight, she longed for something more. Not like winning the lottery or a Cinderella night. She'd be happy with ten minutes to enjoy her coffee over an adult discussion about *anything* but her ornery offspring.

Within seconds the evening cloaked her shoulders and a choir of night creatures soothed the errant pound of her thoughts. A gentle breeze, tainted with the smoky scent of burning leaves, lifted the fine hair at her temple and eased the tension in her neck.

Behind her, Ryan followed, not threatening, but not comforting. His energy whirled around her like a weird tornado and she sensed a challenge more than danger. She squared her shoulders before settling into the old swing. Challenges she could manage. In the past five years, she'd become the queen of challenge management. Put a precipice ahead of her and she'd be the first to peek over the edge. She might soil her pants, but by golly, she'd know what awaited her and be prepared to charge forward.

"It's nice out here." Ryan's deep voice pulled her to his presence.

"My piece of solitude." If her inappropriate bubble of laughter surprised him as much as it had her, he had the good manners to ignore it.

Instead, he approached the porch railing and stopped, his long legs wide, shoulders squared, staring into the night. A sadness emanated from him. Something inside her unwrapped and the remnants of anger she'd harbored about Josh's death ebbed. Ryan had followed a strategy and lost Josh, something he'd never be able to forget. Tonight, he'd shown kindness to her boys and her. She'd be grateful for that.

She sipped the warm coffee to stop the caterpillars crawling beneath her skin. Closing her eyes, she pushed against the aging boards. Her boys were okay. She'd gotten a job and a chance to compete for her dream lease. She should feel like Wonder Woman. She didn't.

When the swing shuddered, Ava's eyes snapped open. She'd assumed he'd sit in the adjacent rocker. The quiet atmosphere crackled like a sudden storm brewing over the ocean. She blinked at the sky, inky black with hundreds of stars peeking through the near naked trees.

Above her, the chain creaked and then started a slow rhythmic beat. Two feet separated her from the man who had intruded into her chaotic household. If she moved her hand to the left, her fingers would brush the stiff fabric of his cammies. A longing developed low in her belly and spiraled upward forcing her to acknowledge its presence. Like a woodland animal hiding in the high grass, her senses heightened toward him. Her fingers twitched and extended toward the heat radiating from his body. Her nostrils flared distinguishing his masculine scent from the decaying leaves. Her breath stilled listening for his slightest movement.

"I might have bounced a guy's head against the ground." He laughed, the deep rich sound filled the silence. "Nate's admission was a new one. But I was no saint at that age. Mom swore I grayed her hair before she turned thirty-five."

"Every time I complained about my boys, Mom would say, payback sucks."

"So, what was your boldest act? The thing you'll take to your grave without revealing?"

His voice contained a playful quality to it, like a game of

truth or dare. Although she glanced his way, the shadows hid his features. Still, the smile in his tone beckoned.

Before responding, she checked the screen door, and then whispered, "Dropping out of college. I told the boys I finished the semester." But she hadn't. She'd married Josh and given up her dreams to support his.

"Yeah." He nodded. "Wouldn't want the kiddos to follow your example."

"And yours?"

"Driving my dad's car without a license. My parents were out of town for the day so I took it for a spin."

"Did you get caught?" Ava said happy to step out of the limelight.

"Of course. I drove by my sister, who was sneaking a smoke at the edge of town."

"And she told?"

"After blackmailing me for a few years," he said. "What was your major?"

Ava tucked her legs beneath her, using the movement to frame an answer. The man had an easy way about him. She usually practiced discretion. With Ryan, information seemed to roll off her tongue.

"Art Design."

"Makes sense."

"Really? How so?" This should be good. He didn't know her. Had no clue about her talents.

"The floor." He stretched his arm along the back of the swing—almost touching her shoulder. "The precision cuts you made. Your attention to the wood grain."

Unbelievable. He hadn't given her a huge compliment, but her chest puffed up like she'd won first place in a competition. To be accurate, she'd won a blue ribbon on her second-grade watercolor. Her keepsake box with the fading satin strip resided in the attic. For a second, the urge to take him up the rickety attic stairs, pilfer her secret stash, and share her prize, warred with her good sense.

"I enjoy working with my hands," she said. "I fantasized about attending Savannah College of Art and Design, but we didn't have the money for it."

When he shifted, the swing trembled beneath his weight and sent a tremor through her. She held her breath, but Ryan continued the momentum of the swing at the same easy cadence as his questions. Mercy, she must have been more adult company deprived than she realized, or he was one heck of a listener because his question about art opened a floodgate.

"Sorry." She ended her dissertation on drawing and painting. "The floor adhesive fried my brain. I don't usually babble like a teenaged girl."

When he laughed again, the knot in her belly relaxed.

"I like to learn about people." A quiet intensity had replaced his humorous tone. "Their likes, dislikes, dreams, desires, secrets."

With his deep voice rumbling in her ears, she wanted to snuggle close to him. Press her ear to his chest to feel the vibrations of his speech. Learn *his* secret desires. Learn if he desired her.

Holy crap! She straightened and shook a finger at him. "I'm going to have to keep an eye on you."

"Me?" He leaned his elbows on his knees and his eyes caught the reflection from an interior house light. "I'm swinging and listening. People have two stories. The one they dream about and the one they live."

Although he seemed relaxed, she sensed energy again. Like his questions, the important details lurked beneath the surface. He'd pegged her. There *were* two sides of her. She'd been so wrapped up in raising children, surviving, she'd had little time to think about her desires.

"Good point," she said. "I'll keep that in mind."

When he lifted his shoulders, the swing rocked. The wood beneath her shuddered reminding her of the budding connection stirring between them.

"Buried desires can surface when we least expect them," he said.

"What were yours?" She pressed her fist against her mouth. "Don't answer that. I mean you don't have to answer that. Ugh! Now would be the time to stuff a dirty sock in my mouth."

"I'm not a fan of torture."

"Good comeback." But she didn't laugh. Couldn't with the way he studied her.

Warmth washed her cheeks, and questions cut her mind into a multitude of fragments—some sharp, some softened like the planes of his features.

"You've got an easy manner. I think that's your secret power," she added in a stage whisper.

"Busted."

He moved closer. His voice held a hint of ... interest? Or was she imagining the awareness because that's what she wanted to hear? She squinted at him, regretting her decision to leave the porch light off. The light bill and the unwanted insect attraction seemed like a dumb excuse to sit in the dark with him. However, darkness added to the evening's tranquility and more dangerous—his allure. She needed illumination to keep her mind on track and gauge his expressions, determine the meaning behind his words.

Irritated at the yoyo action of her thoughts, she straightened against the hard wood. The man might draw her faster than water drew mosquitoes, but she had four children to raise.

"So what's the rest of the story? I saw the secret look going around the table."

His heavy exhale cut through the night. Her heart chilled. *Please don't let it be really bad.*

"The girl they were with," he started. "She's military. Her parents are officers and live next door to me."

"Is she a bad influence?"

"No, nothing like that. Talley's a good kid. Mouthy, but usually for good reason."

She picked up on the slight elevation in his deep voice. "Usually?"

"Talley supplied the tomatoes."

The swing creaked at her sudden movement. "Tomatoes? I've warned the boys about eggs. I never dreamed of tomatoes. What was the target, car or house?"

"A bully." Humor laced his deep voice. "The 1968 Porsche 912 Coupe was collateral damage."

"Why couldn't it have been a Ford?" This was going to cost her and her finances were already in the red zone. "So you know the family?"

"It's a Marine. But there's more to the story. He returned from a combat zone and suffered serious burns. He'll recover but rehab's been rough."

Ava tensed, knowing the implications of his simple statement. "And the altercation with the teens and the car didn't help his integration back into civilian life. I'm sorry for your friend and his family. They're going through tough times. I'm also sorry my boys hauled you into this mess. What's the damage?"

"I promised to get the car detailed."

"I guess he wouldn't consider letting the boys—"

"No. They offered to wash and wax the car. You wouldn't believe how that piece of steel with its special paint must be cleaned. Babies should be so lucky."

"But we aren't." When he didn't respond, she said, "Lucky."

"There's only one place Schmidt lets touch his *baby*."

"And it's very expensive," she guessed.

Even in the low lighting, his nod was distinct, not a trace of hesitancy. She shifted, but the pressure from the drama in addition to the physical aches coursed through her body. "I hope you'll take a check. I don't keep a lot of cash at home." *Ha!* Like she even had a lot of cash.

"I've got a better idea. I need landscaping around my place. Your boys could work off their debt to me." He shifted but didn't stand. "With your permission."

Those three words eased the pressure threatening to explode her head. He'd asked, consulted her. Not that it wasn't her right. They were her sons. Still, men typically forgot that important fact—like the male counselor and the principal at Kyle's last school. But not Ryan.

"Granted with gratitude." She stood. "I assume you want them at your place first light on Saturday."

He held out his hand to her emphasizing his lower position. She hesitated. If she touched him, he'd notice her ragged nails and work-roughened skin. She shook it off. Widows with four children didn't worry about manicures and soft skin.

She clasped his palm, expecting a firm shake. Yes, his big hand swallowed hers and the callouses on his palm rubbed across her skin. However, the firm grasp ended in a gentle release—a slide of flesh on flesh lasting a beat longer than necessary. Her muscles turned to mush, followed by a hot flash of anger.

A simple handshake could not make her forget. Sure, he smelled good. It had been a while since she'd been exposed to the sweet smell of syrup mingled with wood and man. Not the odor of teen boys, strong enough to paralyze a cat, but a mature, sexy man.

Her breath stilled while her heart stuttered. She should've

turned on the light. Lights, lights, lights! Talk about a broken excuse record. But every cell in her body longed to see his gaze. His eyes were brown. She'd noticed, but she wanted to *see* them. Were they shifty with deceit, sparkling with laughter, serious with intent, hooded with sexuality?

"Yes," he continued. "I project—three boys—depending on their dedication to the work—three maybe four weekend days, tops."

Weekends? She dropped back on the swing. "Okay."

Of course, he'd expect weekends. It wasn't like her boys were hanging around doing nothing. They were in school. She'd been so busy smiling and nodding along with the man—what was the deal with his nodding? The old swing creaked with her sudden move to stand. Ryan followed her lead.

He handed her a card. "My cell and address are on it. I live a few blocks from school. Have the boys arrive one hour after dawn next Saturday."

"They'll hate it." She forced a smile.

"I used to count the hours until the weekend so I could sleep in."

"My boys aren't soft." She waved her arm toward the house and barn. "This place needs its share of repairs. I have them up and ready to work by eight o'clock, even on weekends."

Ryan looked like she'd stomped on his toe. "If you need them, we can postpone. My jungle isn't going anywhere."

"Robeys meet their obligations." She followed him to his SUV. "They'll complain, but they'll be there."

"I'll provide lunch."

She fisted her hands. "That's not necessary."

"Even if they pack a lunch, it won't be enough. It's two miles to my place. I'll make sure they have enough energy to pedal home." His tone was low, vibrating through her. But she didn't detect a challenge. Far from it. The man was staring at her mouth like he was considering a kiss. Instead, he opened the SUV door and tipped his chin. “Evening, ma’am.”

No way, would she play the wimpy woman waiting sadly on the porch while the alpha male drove into the sunset. Ava spun on her heel. But darned the man for causing her numb and tingly lips. And he hadn’t even touched her.

“Mom?”

She dropped her hand to her side. The stinkers had been spying on her.

“I’m glad you waited up.” She pulled the door closed and locked it. “We need to talk. Hope?”

“Sound asleep.” Nate rubbed a hand across his flat abdomen. “Can I grab a snack first?”

“Seriously?” Whit flopped onto the sagging sofa cushions. “We ate all of an hour ago.”

Ava pointed toward the back of the house. “Robey powwow, kitchen table.”

Yes, she sounded like a drill instructor, but too bad. Besides, she needed a moment to breathe. Sitting in the shadows with Ryan Murphy had felt...weird. Like an out-of-body experience. She didn’t like it, especially in such a critical time.

Although Whit had ribbed Nate about his appetite, he and Kyle fixed huge peanut butter sandwiches and poured large glasses of milk, which meant she’d need to stop at the store on her way home tomorrow. She brewed a cup of tea and joined her boys, wolfing down sandwiches like they hadn’t eaten since breakfast.

“I’m not rehashing your latest altercation. For the next two weekends, the three of you will help clear Major Murphy’s lot.”

“Mom!” Kyle yelled.

“Don’t wake up your sister,” Ava said.

"You made an agreement with him, without us?" Kyle lowered his voice to a harsh whisper.

"Because of something you three did." Ava winced at her harsh tone. However, if Kyle wanted to be treated like an adult, he needed to act like one. "We made the final cut in the lease competition. If we complete the College property renovations on deadline, the Main Street lease is ours. But we must be first to meet the deadline."

Whit pumped his fist. "Yes."

"Good news for a change." Kyle wiped peanut butter from the side of his mouth. "What did you end up bidding?"

Leave it to her oldest to zero in on the money. But the boys had a right to know. She gave them the amount.

Whit wiped his mouth and swallowed. "Aw Mom, that's slave wages."

"It's start-up money for Robey's Rewards." She held Kyle's angry gaze. "But it's hard to meet our deadline when you three are working somewhere else."

Whit and Nate studied the scars on the long plank table. Although Kyle met her toe-to-toe, his hard gaze softened. "I've got money saved."

"Me too," Whit said.

Nate's gaze darted from one brother to the next. "Why are you looking at me? I haven't been able to get jobs like you."

"No," Whit said. "You spend every spare nickel on food."

Ava held up her hand. "Boys. Since we can't afford the detail cost on the Colonel's fancy car, let it go. Be grateful the Major agreed to barter. In the meantime, we suck it up and do what we can."

"How long will it take to paint and clean the floors?" Kyle said.

Ava sipped her tea, letting the warm liquid ease her frayed nerves. Maybe she'd treat herself to a bubble bath before the real labor started. "Mr. Butler said the last tenant left a lot of trash inside."

"You haven't seen it since the tenant vacated?" Kyle's incredulous tone reminded her of a serious omission. She'd tried. But first the tenant and then Mr. Butler had been unavailable.

"There hasn't been a lease available on Main Street since the Opera House was renovated," she said. "This is our dream. We had to go for it."

"So, we'll deal with it," Whit said.

"Not if we're working for the Major." Kyle's anger had flared back to life. "Tell him we need an extension. By the time we finish with Butler's place, maybe he'll get tired of waiting and do the work or forget about our debt."

Thwack! Ava's teacup jittered on the floor. She hadn't broken the cup, but the hot water burned her fingers. "Your father didn't make a lot of money. But we paid our bills. And we," she swung her finger in an arc to include each youth. "are not going to renege on my word to Major Ryan."

From under the table, Toby pushed his nose against her thigh and whined. Ava stroked his sleek muzzle, soothed by his solid presence.

The wall clock ticked in the silence and the refrigerator hummed. Whit lifted his face to hers, first. Nate followed. After a moment, Kyle met her gaze. Anger hummed from his stiff shoulders, but he jerked his chin down.

She released the breath she'd held.

"I'll purchase supplies tomorrow and prep the place to paint over the weekend. I'll work during the day. Monday after school, you start helping me."

From the way their faces fell, she guessed they'd made afterschool plans for next week. Although her stomach squeezed, she couldn't relent—not if she wanted to open Robey's Rewards.

"If we win, we can open Robey's Rewards before Christmas," she said. "That should be our busiest season for the shop."

"What about the three pieces in the barn?" Whit pushed his empty plate aside. "If you don't finish them, we won't have anything to sell."

"Priorities." She hoped her tone didn't sound as discouraging to them as it did to her. "We'll have to make it work. I can bring a piece inside and paint at night."

"Why did you take him on the porch?" Although he'd lowered the volume, anger still laced Kyle's voice. "In the dark?"

She didn't like his implication, but she didn't like a lot of what came out of her oldest son.

"We had a cup of coffee and discussed a repayment plan we could afford." She didn't blink. "Do you have a problem with that?"

"Maybe," Kyle said.

"He ... stood up ... for us," Whit said, his language problem more pronounced under stress. "He didn't have to, but he did. Talley says he's okay."

"Talley's dad didn't serve with him," Kyle shot back.

Ava stood. "It's been a long night."

And she didn't want to argue with her sons or focus on Ryan. She also didn't want to admit to her family she had reservations about the man. He confused her, made her question her decisions, her perceptions of Josh and his job. Besides, this was Josh's night. He'd been a good husband and father. Thoughts about Ryan seemed like a betrayal. That's what scared her most.

CHAPTER FOUR

Saturday morning Ryan sipped his bold brew and paced the street in front of his manicured lawn. The Robey boys were late. When his phone broke the silence, he expected Ava's name in the caller ID. Schmidt filled the screen.

"Murphy."

"I got your message about winning the first round." Schmidt's staccato words crackled through his receiver.

"We're assigned the renovations for the site on Boundary Street. We've got six weeks to finish."

Schmidt's low curse echoed in Ryan's ear.

"That didn't sound good." Ryan rubbed at the ache starting behind his right eye. "I assume you conducted a site preview before you submitted your proposal because I've never been inside it."

Silence, which was weird. Schmidt wasn't known for holding his tongue or his opinion. "Anyway, Butler gave me the final list. It's mostly outdoor work: concrete drive, sidewalk, and retention wall. The interior work is minimal. He listed junk removal and a dropdown ceiling."

"About that." Schmidt's voice had lost its sharp edge. "My wound's infected."

Ryan's shoulders drooped. "Sorry to hear that."

"Can you manage alone? Doc says I've got to stay off my feet for another four weeks. But I can't lose this chance. I talked to my wife. She's stoked. If I win that lease, it might pull our marriage out of the tank."

Silence stretched over the line.

"I'll cover for you, but you've got to make an appointment." Ryan held his breath. Schmidt needed to talk to someone. PTSD wasn't something you powered through.

"I knew I could depend on you." But Schmidt's tone didn't inspire confidence. "Just help me get the lease. Lana and I have a plan. The new business will...give me a mission after I retire."

Ryan raked a hand through his hair. So retirement fears were exacerbating his PTSD. "Just saying, talking helped me. When I returned from my last det—" A tremor bunched Ryan's shoulders. "Something was off. I couldn't put my finger on it—Like my life plan no longer fit."

"Murphy."

Ryan stiffened. "Sir?"

"My advice? Keep that touchy feely shit to yourself. You don't want *labels* on your record. I know some officers push the programs. I'm not one of them. I'm retiring clean. In the meantime, happy wife means happy life. Help me win that lease."

Ryan stuffed his phone in his pocket. Under normal circumstances, he'd ask Marines to help. But the competition terms stipulated no changes in listed laborers. Like a list existed. It was him and Schmidt.

Nothing like starting a competition down a man. Too bad he'd agreed to let the Robey boys work off their debt. That agreement would cost him at least two days, maybe three day's work on Boundary. With his commitments and his work on base, his competitor better be slow. In the meantime, he'd whip Ava's boys into disciplined young men—or at least working men.

He turned his wrist. Speaking of the Robey boys, they were late, again.

The sun topped the eastern horizon and splintered wispy clouds in deep shades of pink and orange. Except for the rustle of the last of the leaves, nothing moved on the street leading to his drive.

He huffed out a breath. It figured. Widow Robey had her hands full. *Widow Robey?* His lip twitched. Despite the inappropriate label, an image of her in the swing flashed in his head. She'd smiled, almost laughed, unlike the day he'd stood by the chaplain.

His fingers tightened around the mug. There'd been chaos in the Robey household that day too. But everything had stopped the minute Ava had opened the door. His mouth dried. Nothing worse than having to witness the color and spirit drain out of a person.

He turned his wrist, again. 7:04 A.M.

"The later you are. The harder you'll work." Ryan tossed the last of his coffee into the grass.

By the time he'd rinsed his cup, the doorbell rang. On his step stood the three miscreants he planned to turn into respectable citizens—if possible. Kyle, the troublemaker, still held his anger close and tight like a weapon. Whit appeared lost. At first glance, the kid looked like he was one peg short in the wheelhouse department. And that's where the average man went wrong. Behind the vacant look, Whit was watching, listening, preparing for an encounter.

Standing behind his brothers, Nate the follower, shifted his weight from right foot to left. Nervous, no doubt. *Good.* He should be and so should his brothers. Today, intelligence and cunning would get them nowhere. For his job they'd need stamina. The dilemma had cost him a good night's sleep, but he'd come to a decision. Ava had stirred his interest and caused his judgement error. She didn't need a date. She needed help snapping her boys into shape. He was the man for the job.

The storm door groaned from the force of his push. "You're late. I'll take that time off your lunch break."

"Slave labor," Kyle muttered.

Ryan moved into Kyle's personal space, forcing the kid to look up at him. Most men stepped back or looked down when Ryan crowded them. But not Kyle Robey. In different circumstances, Ryan would've cuffed the kid on the shoulder. Sergeant Robey had left a stamp on this kid.

"If you've got something to say, you can address me as Major or sir." He dropped his chin so he was one inch from Kyle's nose. "A man doesn't mumble. He speaks in a clear, respectful tone. Otherwise, all I hear is whining, like a snot-nosed kid."

The anger in Kyle's dark eyes flared, but he held Ryan's stare. "Sir." His tone sounded more snarl than speaking voice. "You're using us as slave labor."

"Opinion noted."

Ryan led the way across his back lawn toward the woods. Shaded by tall pines, the natural area gave way to heavy brush, downed trees, and vines. Under foot, the ground turned boggy. Behind him the boys fought their way through the vegetation.

He stopped by a stake topped with a yellow flag. "This is my property line." He waved his arm toward the north. "That big hardwood tree marks the end of my land. I want you to clear from here to that tree."

Whispered voices broke the silence.

"Does someone have an opinion?" he called.

"We need a machete," Whit volunteered.

"I didn't hear you," Ryan said in his best drill instructor voice.

"We need tools, sir," Kyle responded.

Ryan hid a smile. The kid caught on fast. His plan might work—if Widow Robey didn't bail them out. That was the problem. She was too soft on the boys and they'd started testing boundaries.

At the tool shed behind his house, Ryan pulled out loppers, a hoe, a scythe, and a shovel. No machete or other dangerous tools. He provided specific instructions and then turned to leave. "I'll be back for your morning break. There's a cooler of water on the back porch. Talley's mom, Colonel Frost is home next door. If you need something before I return, ask her."

This time not one complaint broke the silence. His bet, they'd wait until he left. Now, he needed to straighten out Widow Robey.

Difficult mission or mission impossible. He shifted into park and studied the old farmhouse with its wrap-around porch, peeling paint, and sagging roofline. She needed the boys to work *here*.

The dog woofed once from the porch but didn't stand.

Ryan pulled the saw from his vehicle cargo area. "Some guard dog."

Ava opened the door, her dark hair tied beneath her usual Marine bandana. Somehow, she made coveralls look sexy. He shook his head to clear the crazy thought. The dog gave him a long glance.

"Major Murphy?"

He frowned. So much for their agreement to call him Ryan. Two could play this game. "Ma'am."

"The boys left on time." She lifted one eyebrow. "Were there problems on your end?"

Affirmative, but it had nothing to do with her sons. "No. I put them to work."

She waited, her eyes huge in her small face. He liked patient Marines. It showed confidence and motivation to learn. And women?

He lifted the saw. "I noticed the drag on your front door last night. Thought I'd cut it off so it will swing free and won't damage your new floor."

She stepped back to admit him. "I've already trimmed the excess. But I could use help hanging it."

Okay, Widow Robey didn't need help—except with her sons. Behind Ava, the front door rested on two old sawhorses. Shavings peppered the wood floor. In the background an old rock tune played. The scent of fresh coffee, wood, and woman tickled his nose. He should've stayed home and supervised the boys.

She lifted an ancient planer, the ball rusty with age. "Mr. Oakes sharpened my tools in exchange for two pies a few months ago."

He stood the door in front of the frame and lifted it onto the hinges. "What kind?"

With a gentle tap of a hammer, she lined up the top hinge and dropped in the peg. Those incredible eyes met his. Today, flecks of gray dominated her eye color.

"Apple and banana cream," she said.

Coffee scented her breath. *Look away.* He didn't. "Homemade?"

Her smile sizzled him like a steak on a hot grill.

"Of course. Hope and I made them. She loves to help in the kitchen—when Whit lets her."

She dropped to her knees to tap in the bottom hinge and he breathed. Kids. Widow Robey had four of them. Package deal. *Keep that in mind, Marine.*

She stood. "Why are you here?"

When he turned to her, the welcoming smile had faded and the wide-eyed gaze that had sent his mind on a detour had hardened.

"Guilt." He met her toe to toe. "You're trying to fix up the place. I took your labor force."

When her fists traveled to her hips, he breathed. For a moment, she looked like she was going to punch him. The right side of his mouth lifted. Her eyes narrowed and he compressed his lips. She didn't miss a thing.

"I pay my debts." She narrowed those pretty eyes until he could swear they transmitted a death ray. "I don't need pity. I need stuff."

"Stuff." The word elongated with the spin of his thoughts.

You'd think he'd be used to her smile by now, but it did a number on his insides. Not the same as the gut-churning fear of riding through a village of hidden hostiles. More like the first time he'd jumped from a plane. Scary and exhilarating at the same time. With a jump, you prayed your chute would open so you didn't crash into the earth. With Ava, he prayed she wouldn't shoot him down before he made a move. His throat closed and he croaked like the big bullfrogs he used to catch along the river.

"I'm opening a shop selling furniture," she was saying. "I refinish good wood. Sometimes I paint scenes." She shrugged and looked at the floor. "I can also reupholster sofas and chairs. With the base nearby in Jacksonville, I figured there would be a need."

Where was his head? She had four mouths to feed on a survivor's income. Of course, she needed money. And he drives onto her farm with a saw.

"Sounds like a solid plan." He gave her a nod of encouragement. "Jacksonville's full of resale shops, but most are junk stores. Inexpensive nice things are hard to come by."

She placed the tools in an old wooden toolbox like his

Grandpa used. In a way the box fit her. She wasn't shiny like the red two-tiered metal box he kept in the garage. Life had weathered her, but she'd remained steady, reliable, interesting.

"I remember." She stood. "Josh and I rented a place when he was stationed at Lejeune."

He stacked the two sawhorses and followed her outside to the back of the house. Down a dirt lane an ancient barn squatted to the right. With its huge sliding door dangling from one hinge, the building looked in worse shape than the house nestled in the trees.

Instead of following the path to the barn, Ava continued around the house. Four warped wooden steps led to a large enclosed back porch. She climbed in front of him, her hips swinging side to side.

Sweat beaded his forehead and slickened his palms. He tightened his grip on the wood. When she smiled and held the screen door open, he focused on the door frame, maneuvering the sawhorses through the narrow opening—anything to keep his focus from the way her eyes crinkled at the corners.

His head spun like he'd guzzled too many beers. "So, you're interested in reusable furniture?"

She waved toward the right, an obvious work area with articles of furniture crammed in the corner. Standing alone, a three-drawer chest, the apparent work in progress, had been sanded and awaited a finish. Behind it stood a long skinny table with a Sunberry scene painted across the top.

He placed the sawhorses in an opening near the screen and approached the table. "Did you paint the clock tower?"

Ava ran her fingertips along the surface. "I finished last Thursday. I've done geometric designs and stencils, but this is the first scene."

"I'm impressed. I can't draw stick figures."

Color bloomed on her cheeks. "It came out better than I'd hoped."

"Amazing detail." He traced the opera house with its signature clock tower to keep from touching her cheek. "It looks like the downtown area."

"Thanks. Mom got me started." She stooped near a box of papers and lifted the cover to a pad. "I took a photo and then sketched this before I started painting."

He'd come to help her out and talk about her sons. Instead, he wanted to know about her. What she liked. What she wanted. He moved closer. Although she was more than a head shorter than he was, a hint of wood and cinnamon wafted up from her. Cinnamon rolls were his favorite breakfast treat, but he liked cinnamon flavored oatmeal too.

He leaned closer and stared at the sketch, but the pencil marks didn't penetrate his thoughts. The soft lilt of her voice settled around him. The words acrylic, paint, polyurethane, and shading flashed like flares in the desert of his mind. The sweep of her long slender fingers and the curve of her hands mesmerized him. She didn't polish her nails. Instead, flecks of dirt dotted her nailbeds and a scrape extended along her knuckles.

"I started with a line of elephants on a changing table for Hope," she said.

He straightened, hoping she hadn't caught his stare. "Elephants?"

"Yeah, you know. Like in Dumbo. The little one holds on to the big one's tail."

"I don't have a lot of experience with kid furniture, but Mom's birthday is coming up. Is the table for sale?"

His mother's birthday was in the spring, but she'd like the table. *He'd* like the table, liked the idea of owning something this incredible woman had created with her hands.

"Oh." She elongated the word into two syllables.

Did she have any idea how cute she was with her lips puckered in surprise? He stepped back.

"I planned to sell it." She ran a fingertip along the furniture's edge. "But I need a piece to show an example of my work."

"I'll give you a deposit to hold it for me. You keep it until you paint another one. When you've created a replacement piece, we'll settle, and I'll take it home."

He could watch the way her facial expressions transformed all day long, especially with the morning light dappling her flesh. Unaware of his scrutiny, she stared at the furniture in question, scrunched up her nose, and manipulated her mouth like she was trying to extract a fishbone from a piece of meat.

"It's hand-painted, you know." She still avoided his gaze.

Duh! She'd spent the last ten minutes explaining her process. Pricing her work obviously caused her heartburn.

"I spent almost a week on the piece, and that doesn't include the time to get the right photo. I took a picture of the clock tower in the morning and evening on sunny and cloudy days. Cloudy days were the hardest because the sun shines most of the time."

At this rate she sounded like she'd priced a piece of wood close to the National Debt. He shifted his weight to the other foot and refolded his arms. *Wait for it.*

"However—" She turned to meet him. "I'll discount it because you agreed to let me keep it for display. Nine hundred dollars. And it's good wood."

"Would two-fifty be a fair deposit?" He struggled to maintain a straight face.

Her shoulders dropped like she'd released her pack after a five-mile run, and then she thrust out her hand. "Sold."

With the detours his mind had taken, the last thing he needed was to accept her handshake, but he couldn't get around it. He gave her an abrupt pump and released her before he did something they'd both regret.

"So, you need furniture for more scenes?"

"I can't buy anything right now, but I'm open to donations." She grinned. "I'll even pick it up. I've got an old flatbed trailer for items too big for my Explorer."

The rush of her words grounded him. Her sacrifices to make her dreams a reality mirrored the reason he planned to stay in the Marines for the full ride. Money couldn't buy a dream. Dreams clung to your soul. His thoughts halted right along with his breathing. Images of her lingered in his mind.

"Don't get me wrong. We're not starving," she was saying, unaware of his lack of attention. "But if you happened to mention it to your men or around town, I'd appreciate it."

He'd appreciate kissing her. No, he needed a break—from her. Before he made a critical misstep.

He turned his wrist. "I better check on the boys. I've got a few contacts at the base and my mom is in the Sunberry Junior League. Telling Mom produces better results than a full-page ad in the local newspaper."

"I'll take all the press I can get." Her smile could light the room.

He halted, his hand on the screen door. "A few minutes ago you got prickly when I mentioned helping you out." His voice had a strangled quality to it, but the woman messed with his head, cranked him up worse than last year's generator.

"I don't mean to aggravate you." He should shut up, but he needed to say something to make her talk to him, kick him out of her house, anything but stare at him with soulful heart-penetrating eyes.

"I get you're a proud woman. I'm not trying to take that away. I admire you." Heat oozed up his neck. "I want to give you a hand. Help on the jobs you can't do. Can you let me do that for you?"

She released a breath, but that didn't mean she would agree. Suspicion still narrowed those beautiful eyes, now looking greener than gray.

"Provide an example of such a job," she said.

"That's up to you," he said, sensing victory or at least a partial one.

She continued to stare him down, but he didn't look away. She didn't blink. Neither did he. Although he'd been trained by the best the U.S. had to offer, she matched his glare second for second.

After a moment she wagged her index finger like she was scolding the dog. A ridiculous urge to laugh almost messed up his hard look, but he'd spent his first nineteen years with two sisters. Ava was caving in. He had to hold out a little longer.

"Around the farm, okay." She huffed out a breath. "Did you ever build something with your dad?"

Women. One minute they were negotiating. The next minute it was freaking story time.

"Like a clubhouse or something?" he asked.

"Yeah. Something you and your dad built together."

"A clubhouse." That had been an amazing summer. No sisters to aggravate him. Dad had taught him how to frame a building. Crap! She was staring at him again.

"It's behind a big magnolia at my mother's house." He cringed. Man, he sounded like such a loser. "I thought it was the coolest place when we finished. Sometimes I'd spend the night out there. It was my place—away from my sisters and their friends."

"Exactly." She nodded. "Building that clubhouse with your dad made it special. The work bonded you. Something you did together. That's what I want for my sons. We're working on a special project, a family business. Josh can't be here with them, but I can."

She had a crazy way of expressing ideas, but he understood this project was off-limits and it made sense why she felt that way.

"I admit I'm over the top when it comes to my independence," she said. "I'm not trying to be unreasonable. But our family business is special. I want my boys to be proud of something they built with their own hands. I want them to have good memories about that work like you have about your clubhouse."

She jerked open the back door, and he followed her through the house to the front porch. The railing wobbled under his hand. When his free time opened, he'd make a trip to the farm and fix her handrail—with or without her permission.

"Major?"

He dropped his chin but tried not to glare at her. "I thought we had the name discussion."

She thrust out her hand to him. "Thanks. Ryan."

She added his name in a whispery voice causing all kinds of inappropriate reactions south of the border. That look again. His mind snagged on the tilt of her face, the curve of her jaw. She moistened her lips, and he leaned toward her.

"Mom! We need help!" Nate skidded his bike to a stop. "The chain flew off and cut Kyle."

CHAPTER FIVE

At the hospital Ava rushed to the admission desk. She'd lost Josh and Mom. She couldn't lose Kyle—not her strong, belligerent first-born.

"Kyle Robey." Ava cringed. She sounded like a strangled cat.

Her heart pounded ten times faster than the technician clicked through computer screens. By the time she was ready to reach over the counter and *help* find her son, the man looked at her with a cheery smile. She breathed. No one smiled at a mother if her son suffered a serious injury.

"Looks like he'll need a few stitches." He handed her a clipboard. "After you sign the consent, the physician will fix him up."

A minor cut. He was okay. But he might suffer a serious injury when she took him home. They were supposed to be starting a new business, a new life. Not jacking up the family drama.

Beside her, Ryan swiped at the sweat streaking his forehead. They'd both aged ten years during that race to the hospital. Her shoulders drooped and her vision blackened and then sharpened. Something soft and warm pressed against her back.

"Do you need to sit down?" Ryan murmured near her ear. "I can stay with Kyle for you."

"I'm okay." Although grateful for his presence, her weakness annoyed her. She hadn't gotten weak-kneed since an eighteen-month-old Kyle dove into her stepstool and sliced open his forehead.

Disoriented like she'd been spinning in a circle and suddenly stopped, she followed the technician down the long hall. Ryan walked at her side. Although he didn't wrap his arm around her, his presence infused her with a calm strength. She'd missed the support, someone to stand with her, step in should she need him. But not take over. And Ryan hadn't done that. He respected her wishes, wasn't threatened by her need for independence.

The squeak of her soft-soled shoes echoed in the wide passageway. A baby cried. The wheels of a wheelchair rolled down the hall followed by the ding of an elevator. The tech turned into a large room with three gurneys separated by hanging curtains. To the far right, the white drape had been pulled. The tech motioned them forward.

Although pale, Kyle's dark eyes widened in surprise and then narrowed. Ava scanned his exposed thigh and nodded —fixable.

"Who authorized you to use my chainsaw?" Ryan's deep voice cut through the silence.

"You said to clean up the lot." Even with a four-inch gash on his thigh, Kyle's tone remained in the usual snarl. "You weren't around for a consult."

"Kyle, show the Major respect."

Kyle's head swung from Ryan to her, his features darkening. "Oh, I get it. You went to the house. With us working on your stupid jungle, you had Mom all to yourself." The volume of Kyle's voice raised with the color in his cheeks. "Was that the plan all along?"

Heat raced up Ava's neck. "That's enough."

"I gave you tools and specific orders to follow." Ryan's voice remained steady, despite Kyle's taunt.

"That would've taken all day."

"You *have* all day."

Ava squirmed. Her boys didn't have all day. With her agreement with Butler, they didn't have four days to spare. But Ryan didn't know because she'd remained secretive to avoid his pity. Kyle had paid the price for her.

"Excuse me folks." A woman dressed in a white lab coat raised her voice to carry over the conversation. "I'm Dr. Sanchez. Kyle was lucky. No permanent damage. Mom, Dad, please take a seat in the waiting room. We'll call you as soon as I've closed the wound."

Ava's thoughts buzzed like the countryside during their high-speed ride to the hospital. Between Kyle's accusations and the physician's assumptions, she'd fallen down a rabbit hole without a shred of daylight above. Still, she had obligations to her children.

In the hall she slid her hand along Ryan's arm, ignoring the way his muscles coiled beneath her touch.

"We need to talk."

Unlike her boys and Josh before his death, Ryan didn't question her request. He pressed a calloused hand over hers and squeezed. Strength surged through her. Josh had cherished and protected her but never empowered her. Too bad she wouldn't get more time with Ryan.

He guided her through the sterile hallways like a man on a mission and a man who knew the hospital layout. At the exit, he pushed open the door and followed her to an outdoor eating area for staff and guests. Seven empty tables dotted the patio.

Ava unwrapped her hand from his arm and stepped away. "I apologize for Kyle's disrespectful behavior. Seems like I'm apologizing to you a lot."

Ryan shrugged. "He's got a lot of anger brewing."

"And one of these days he's going to wise off to the wrong man."

A frown furrowed his tanned brow and he straightened making him appear taller. "I don't hit boys."

"No, I didn't expect you would." She moistened her lips. "This was my fault."

"It's the results of a bad decision. Your boy will learn from this and make a better choice next time."

Next time wasn't in her future—not for her and Ryan.

He pulled out a patio chair for her. "You're a good mother, kind and loving."

"But too soft," she finished, dropping like a stone onto the hard mesh seat.

"You stay cool under pressure," Ryan continued, sitting across from her. "I've seen a lot of baseball injuries coaching youth teams. When you combine children, moms, and blood, you get chaos, especially when the moms lose their minds. But not you."

She opened her mouth, but nothing came out. He wasn't being sarcastic or mocking her. His gaze remained steady, intent, and dead serious. Despite Kyle's attitude, despite the chaos, despite everything, he thought she was a good mother.

The right side of his mouth lifted with a hint of amusement and he rubbed his forearm. She followed his movements to the red halfmoons still marking his flesh. Oops. She'd held it together by clawing his skin.

"You were worried." He lifted his shoulders like that was a perfect excuse for drilling his arm with her nails. Thank goodness she wasn't into catclaws.

He huffed out a breath. "I was rattled too. A chainsaw is a wicked tool. And Nate's description—"

His crooked smile tingled the roots of her hair along with a few other choice places.

"But you kept your head, calmed your kids, waited until you had the facts."

The pressure weighting her shoulders disappeared and she gripped the table to keep from floating out of her chair. His praise called for a response, but she didn't want him to stop. Shoot, she could sit all day listening to the man tell her she was wonderful. She might not believe it, but that didn't mean she didn't enjoy it.

"Thank you for saying that," she managed. "Since Josh and Mom passed, I've missed adult approval. I think I do an okay job with my kids. At least—" She dropped his gaze. "I've done my best. They're wonderful kids. But adult validation? Wow! It's like balm to a wound—even if I am a little soft on them."

"You're welcome," he said. "With testosterone surges firing nonstop, you've got your hands full."

The tingles transitioned into a muscle curl deep in her pelvis. She shifted on the uncomfortable chair to conceal her response. So much for the good mom. But it wasn't like she had a kind, supportive man, giving her positive feedback on a regular basis. Especially one with such a sexy mouth. Ava cleared her throat.

"I have three rambunctious boys," she said. "Superglue can do amazing things on cuts."

When he straightened, she bit the inside of her cheek to keep from grinning. The thought had been random, but it was the only thing that came to her other than talking about what he'd look like shirtless. Besides, she loved surprising him. Loved his praise more. She swallowed. The more time she spent with Ryan, the more she admired him.

"I've kind of glued a few cuts together." She wrinkled her

nose at the memory of those gashes. "It's cheaper and less traumatic than stitches."

"Cool under pressure and innovative." He winked. "Your attributes keep stacking up."

"Flattery goes a long way with single moms." She thumped her forehead with the heel of her hand. "Sorry. This is not me. I'm a mom and I need to concentrate on my job."

But staying focused was *really* hard when his dark eyes twinkled like that.

"Like I said. There's nothing wrong with the job you're doing. But with three boys, a person could get overwhelmed. That's why I offered to help." He chewed his lip. "I'd like to work with your boys."

She felt as if the last train out of nowhere had rolled from the station and she'd missed it. Although she couldn't accept his offer, this strong, considerate man understood the value of her sons. She'd take that as a win. Her boys, especially Kyle, were not a total loss. But a relationship between her and Ryan could never work. Whit and Nate might come around. But even if she forced Kyle to give Ryan a chance, her first born would always see Ryan as trying to replace his father.

"I appreciate your offer. They're good boys. And Kyle's not lazy," she blurted out the words before she changed her mind.

Life hadn't been easy, but she'd come to terms with the decisions she'd made, sometimes had to make. However, this one hung in her chest like the autumn leaves clung to trees—knowing the fall was inevitable but holding on for the last shred of hope. She pulled her shoulders back and let go of possibility—for her. At least she didn't have to reveal why her boys deserved a pass. How Kyle had helped her out of bed when she couldn't do it herself. How three small boys had pulled her through days so dark that putting on clean clothes was almost beyond her. And that didn't even begin to cover caring for a baby sister.

"He was hurrying to help me," she finished. "We put our family project on hold while they work off their obligation to you."

Ryan looked like she'd popped him with a pin to release his tension. He dropped his chin and did that crazy bobbing thing he did.

"I told you we could postpone the work."

"A postponement wouldn't have helped," she said. "Plus, I wanted my sons to be accountable for their actions."

"If I had known—"

"You would've kept a closer eye on them." She took in a slow steadying breath and focused on maintaining a reasonable tone. "I get that. And I appreciate your offer."

"But you won't let me help?" he said, his expressive gaze piercing her soul.

"It's too complicated." She hoped he'd let it go. Hoped he wouldn't force her to reveal the horrendous issue for her sons.

"So we call it even and I stand down."

He didn't look happy with the resolution. His jaw bunched and she braced for a debate. But he didn't speak. Didn't push. He sat silent as a stone assessing her with those amazing dark eyes.

She admired his restraint. From the continued tic in his square jaw, she guessed he had a lot to say on the subject. Someone had taught the man patience. According to talk at the Sunberry diner, his mother Stella was a force of nature. Someday she'd like to meet the woman. After today, she doubted that someday would arrive.

"Comments?" she prompted.

"What about us? You and me."

Her sharp intake pierced the silence. The words *you and me* darted through her brain like birds diving for midair insects. It wasn't just her. He'd also felt the connection between them. She loved her role as a mother. Loved her children. But sometimes...sometimes she wanted to be a woman. Wanted a man to look at her with desire in his eyes. Wanted to be free to enjoy life—if only for an evening. Just one. And her wants and needs came second behind the most important four people in her life.

Unable to force the explanation past her lips, she studied him. She didn't want to tell him, didn't want to stop what had started. Her wants didn't count.

"I'm sorry, but this won't work," she whispered.

A muscle in his jaw twitched and he rubbed the flat of his hand over his chest, moving it back and forth like he was massaging a sore muscle. He held her gaze. Patient. Silent.

Her scalp tingled, but she forced the words out. "I was wrong. If I led you to believe—" Crap, spit it out. "It's been enough time since Josh died. And you're a kind, attractive man. But it won't work."

"So you felt something too?" His wonderful low voice vibrated through her.

"The minute we talked on the porch." She cringed at the breathless quality in her voice. "I didn't even know I wanted a relationship with another man. I've been so busy trying to keep my head above water. But you—"

Wonder opened her eyes like the first time she'd witnessed a butterfly emerge from a chrysalis. He made her feel pretty, sensual, desired. But it was more than that. Far more. She swallowed, wishing she'd brought a bottle of water.

When Ryan looked at her, her fingers tingled to touch him. Be touched. Connect with a man. This man.

He held out his hand to her. "Let me help you. Let's see where this goes."

Every fiber in her body leaned toward him and she tightened her hands into fists to keep from tracing the callouses creasing his palm, to resist what he offered.

Squeezing her eyes closed, she shook her head. "I wish I could. But Josh reported to you. He died on your watch. I understand. I don't hold you responsible."

"I—"

"It doesn't matter and it won't matter to my sons. I'm not going to ask them to forgive you. I don't want them to have to consider it. To have to make that decision. My children have already survived too many hardships. It's my job to shelter them from more."

She tapped her phone to display the time. "I better get back inside."

When he pulled open the door for her, pain shadowed his dark eyes and hardened his jaw. She touched his cheek and a muscle beneath her fingers bunched.

"I'm sorry my words were harsh. I know how hard your job is because I lived it with Josh. You've served at a terrible cost to your soul too. I don't think there's a way to go where you've been without paying that price. So thank you. Thank you for the sacrifices you've made to keep me and my boys safe. Thank you for helping me. But as soon as their work is finished, I can't— We can't see one another."

CHAPTER SIX

RYAN HAD LOST THE BATTLE, BUT HE WOULDN'T SURRENDER the war.

The SUV's powerful engine roared beneath his boot, but his cargo, Ava and company, were too distracted to notice. Avoiding Ava in the navigator seat, he glanced in the rearview. Kyle glared his way. He couldn't blame the kid. He was trying to help his mother and Ryan was the unwitting obstacle.

On the twenty-mile drive to Ava's place, he worked the problem like a corroded cable from an old battery. He'd honor her need to keep her project in the family. He'd honor her request to keep her at an emotional distance. But helping her around the farm was open territory—whether she liked it or not.

When he stopped in the Robey drive, Ava turned to the three boys lining the second seat. "Nate, Whit, help Kyle inside. Once he's settled, I want you back here. Nate load your bike. You and Whit will ride home from the Major's as planned. Whit get Kyle's cell phone out of the top right-hand drawer of my desk. It should be charged and ready to go."

"That's not necessary."

"Major." She narrowed her eyes. "I'm giving the orders here."

He almost bit a hole on the inside of his lip, but he didn't grin. He didn't even twitch his lip. Not with her staring him down.

"Boys!" Her voice cracked through the vehicle like a rifle shot.

"Are you mad at me?" Hope asked in a small voice from her place in the third seat.

"No sweetie. I need your help."

Ryan cleared his throat. The woman had the mom thing down. While the boys rumbled around the Robey family like thunder clouds, Hope brought the sunshine. One smile from the tot and he was convinced everything would work out. Stupid, but he couldn't help but return her grin in the rearview.

"Can you nurse Kyle?" Ava was saying, her features tender with love. "You know. Get him a pillow and something to drink."

Ryan's heart accelerated. Ava also had the compassion thing down. Those doe eyes made his knees ready to bend at her feet. Better yet.... *Back it down, Marine.* Removing the woman from his mind was like trying to clean up a third world country. Every time he'd compartmentalized one trait, she blew his mind up with another intriguing characteristic.

Package deal. Hands off.

For now, he needed to maintain his focus on Ava and her family's needs. Which was exhausting. No wonder she looked tired. He was drained following her unit's escapades after three encounters. A fight, a tomato fallout, and now an injury. The Robey kids were a continuous mine field. And Ava developed a well-laid tactical plan despite the chaos.

"I can do that." Hope's sweet voice filtered through his thoughts. "I'm a good nurse."

Now he got it. Solid Marines created families to stabilize their lives. A child's voice eased a man's rough edges, especially after a tough deployment.

Within seconds, Hope pushed open the door, slid onto the ground, and was tearing up the front porch steps, eager to grant her mother's wish. Ava's gentle touch on his arm jolted his attention to her. He turned toward her, shifting in the cramped bucket seat.

"My sons are twelve, fourteen and fifteen. They are not Marines. They are boys. They're pretty good workers but need adult supervision."

"You're right." He ran his hands along the sides of his mouth, hoping he didn't wear the same besotted expression on his face as her daughter had worn moments ago. "I should've locked the tool shed and monitored them closer."

Sadness tipped her smile. "I should've filled you in about our project."

He grunted. Earning a Marine's trust had come easy to him. Looked like Ava would require more convincing. And he'd better get up for the job.

"We acquired a family job." She scratched her cuticle with her thumbnail. "The money we earn goes toward our new business. My boys know this and are anxious to finish your yard work."

When she looked up at him, her features softened. His stupid heart started a double-time exercise. While she chewed her bottom lip, his tongue tingled. Would she let him kiss her? Would she taste like coffee? Might tick her off, but it might be worth the chance.

"I'll take Kyle's place."

What the— A breath whistled from his mouth. "No way."

She wagged a slender finger at him. "It's the perfect solution. Bennie lives a mile down the road. I'll ask him to come over and help out with Kyle."

"Do you think I'm going to stand around while you perform the grunt-work behind my house?"

Although the woman had lost her mind, every muscle in his body hit ready status. Talking to her was like racing from a skirmish to a firefight with her waving the battle flag. She leaned over the console and her scent beckoned. Fire glittered in her hazel eyes and her nostrils flared. The crazy urge to kiss her senseless intensified.

"I work as hard as my son or a man," she challenged.

"There's one problem with your perfect solutions." He jabbed his chest with his thumb and pulled his gaze from her full upper lip. "Me. Marines work as a unit. That's how we survive in theatre. We use the same strategy in life."

"You are not in the Robey unit."

But he wanted to be. "Marines count on one another to guard their backs. By helping you, I'm guarding Josh's back."

She did a quirky twisty thing with her mouth and then huffed out a breath. When his sisters did that, they were processing a decision. He'd rarely liked it, but it always came. His bet, Ava would slam him with hers in a few seconds.

"We need to get this out of the way right now."

Uh-oh, sounded like her words were more for her benefit than his.

"It was hard losing Josh. It was harder starting again. But I did it and I'm proud of it." With each word her voice strengthened. "I'm not weak and I don't need a Marine to save the day for me."

"No ma'am." He shook his head. "You're far from weak. I'd say you're about the toughest woman I know, not counting my mother. And you're neck and neck with her."

Her eyes were still narrowed, but a wisp of a smile creased her lips. "Excellent. Then we understand one another."

He touched her forearm. "Not quite. You were adamant

about paying your debt to me." He struggled to keep his voice soft. "It works both ways."

"Except you don't owe me anything."

"My debt is to Sergeant Robey. The XO—" he moistened his lip. "Sorry. The executive officer at Lejeune is responsible for family readiness. When a unit is deployed, the XO cares for the families left behind. I'm the XO."

"Josh isn't deployed." She hesitated, and the pain of loss shadowed her gaze, even after five years.

"My negligence." His words scraped the back of his throat. "I promised I'd look out for his family."

"That's thoughtful, but like I said, I can take care of my family."

"That's not the only reason." He'd made a lot of speeches, but they were simple compared to what he had to say. Matter of a fact, this was as hard as accompanying the chaplain during notifications. He moved closer. The urge to take her in his arms tingled through his biceps, which wasn't the kind of care Robey had in mind when he'd last talked to Ryan.

"I didn't offer to help you because I think you're weak or pity you. I offered because Robey died for his country. I offered because I'm a Marine and it's a privilege and an honor to give back to a man and his family who have paid the ultimate price. Now, you can accept my help or you can fight me. But I'm not going to stop."

He couldn't stop even if he wanted to because the woman had gotten to him. This stubborn, proud, amazing woman had ambushed him. The loud rasp of his breaths filled the silence. He swallowed trying to slow the pound of his heart and control his labored breathing. The crazy thing was, he liked every minute of it. Liked her even more.

"Let it go Ryan," she whispered. "Put Josh's cross down. You've done your part and I'm grateful."

He held up his hand, thankful it wasn't visibly shaking.

Because the words threatening to pour from him scared the bejesus out of him. Scared him worse than combat. But secrets led to destruction. Success only came through communication.

"It's more than my debt to Josh." His words rushed out on a ragged exhale.

She folded her arms across her chest. Something about the woman tripped him up. Which never happened. He'd been to the freaking combat zone three times. He didn't lose his cool. In his line of work, men who lost focus ended up dead. But that didn't change the burning in his lungs like he'd survived an explosion. He coughed.

"You told me you *had* to start the family business." He needed a drink of water. "Helping you get your family acclimated to Sunberry is like that for me."

"That's noble of you, but—"

"You don't understand. It's not an option. It's something I *have* to do."

Until he'd heard the ring of his own words, he hadn't understood the depth of his commitment to her. He still wasn't one hundred percent sure of his motivation. But he couldn't back down, couldn't walk away. Something about this woman, this family, filled the empty hole that had plagued him since he'd come home.

Although she'd uncrossed her arms, worry lines marred her forehead. He needed to put distance between them, but that wasn't an option. The interior of the SUV closed in. Dried red paint smudged her cuticle. He fisted his hands to keep from tracing her skin with his finger.

"So you can shut me down, give me orders, or whatever you need to do to sustain that streak of independence driving you," he murmured. "But you're not getting rid of me."

"I won't let you jeopardize my relationship with my sons."

"Understood." A mother should guard that bond, like a

man guarded the relationship with a woman—even a budding relationship. A spark had arced through him the moment he'd walked into her old farmhouse. He planned to follow it, see where it led.

When Ava turned to him, he squared his shoulders. He couldn't let those doe eyes get to him. If he was going to help her, he had to stand his ground. Besides, abandoning Ava was like abandoning his principles.

"On the porch...today—" She clasped her hands together and bumped them against her chin. "I thought.... I wanted to be a regular single woman, open to relationships, maybe even go on a date. But I can't, at least not now."

Desire pulled him nearer. "You're a beautiful woman, inside and out. Which is hard to come by. Your boys are lucky to have you and will learn from your example."

Longing burned in her gaze and it fueled his craving for her. But he wouldn't disrespect her. He placed his hand on the console, palm up. Dad told him to always do the honorable thing. Sometimes it was hard. Mom taught him patience, especially for important things, important people. Ava placed her trembling hand in his, sending a laser of energy straight through him. The urge to free her hair from the bandana and pull her so close they'd meld into one unit, flesh on flesh, surged through him. He squeezed her hand.

"I'm a patient man. I want to be with you, ride this thing between us until the end, see where it leads." He traced her lip with his thumb and then huffed out a breath. "Damn woman, I want to kiss you senseless. Have since that night on your porch. But I won't. I'll respect your independence and your stubborn pride. I'll do my best to help your boys, show them how to respect you and themselves. And I'll help you fix up this old farm before it crumbles at your feet. For that, I need one thing."

She was staring at him with those golden eyes full of

wonder. He pulled away, fisting his hands to stifle the urge to do exactly what he'd promised he wouldn't do—kiss her senseless. He'd bet his right nut she'd be full of passion in bed the same as her passion for her family and her business.

"I can't make promises until I know what it is," she whispered.

"Your trust." He fisted his hand. "I'm doing my best to show you I'm an honorable man."

"It's not you I'm worried about." Her smile drooped at the corners of her mouth.

And it wasn't her boys. Ryan swallowed. "You're worried about how you'll react...to me?"

She nodded raising her right brow and sending his libido through the roof.

"So why—"

"Because my family comes before my personal desires. Because our business dream is important to the well-being of this family and Josh's memory. I made that commitment to my family and to myself. Children learn by example."

The stubborn tilt of her chin and the rasp in her voice made it clear. She'd never turn her back on her children the same way he'd never turn his back on a Marine. The heat racing through his body cooled and his thoughts cleared.

Ava had a commitment and so did he. Schmidt was depending on him to come up with the Main Street lease. When he'd stumbled upon Ava and her family, he'd pushed his Schmidt obligation to his B list.

"What's your deadline on the business project?" Ryan asked.

"I hoped to open before Christmas."

"Short fuse."

Her shoulders drooped. "Which is why I need to take Kyle's place."

He shook his head. "Not happening."

"My sons will finish the job." She crossed her arms in front of her chest. "It's not negotiable."

He forced three slow breaths to relieve the pressure in his head. She was so stubborn. And her resolve and fierce determination were two of the traits he admired.

"So you'll let me help you around here?"

"All right already," Ava said. "Farm projects are not off limits."

"Excellent. I'm working on something too." And he'd blown up his schedule. "I'm taking leave to free up more time."

The tension around her mouth relaxed, not completely, but her armor had slipped. And he intended to take advantage of that slip, for both of them.

"And—" he held her gaze captive watching for signs of noncompliance. "You and I are not off the table.

Her mouth worked like a dog eating peanut butter. She was adorable.

"We'll see."

"Not good enough," he said.

"Get over yourself." She rested her fists on her hips. "That's all your getting."

He loved watching her get huffy over a bone of contention. She might be stubborn, but she'd never come up against him. And he planned to get a whole lot more than a *we'll see*.

CHAPTER SEVEN

"Romance is not in the Robey plan," she muttered as Ryan's SUV turned and disappeared onto the highway. That man was trouble. Age-old sexual attraction settled low in her belly. Short on funds, labor, and time, this was no time to let desires supersede her plan. Still... A smile tipped her lips. No one could fault a guy for trying. Or a woman from daydreaming.

Ava's smile stayed in place until she unlocked the door to the College Street property and the musty scent of garbage, old newspapers, and dust filled her nostrils. Her shoulders slumped lower as she rotated inside the back door.

"My price for renovation was too stinking low."

A smart woman would've checked the property again before making an offer. A smart woman would never let her emotions rule her business sense. A smart woman worked instead of whined.

Her judgement had taken a holiday. On their best day her wonderful boys couldn't get through this mess. She needed a unit, or better yet a battalion, to remove the debris. And that was before the improvements she'd promised started. No wonder she'd won the first round.

She squared her shoulders. Josh hadn't given up. Mom hadn't given up. They'd lost their lives, but they'd *never* lost heart.

"I won't quit," she whispered to the scarred walls. "I won't quit." She raised her voice. "I won't quit!"

Her competition better be comparable to two college grads who were long on dream and short on know-how.

Two hours later, Ava lobbed her final bag of trash, for the first room, into the dumpster and dusted her hands. She pumped her fist and then glanced around to ensure no one had witnessed her behavior. But hey, nothing like a job accomplished to bolster a gal's strength. Besides, a self-confidence wobble carried no shame if her kids didn't witness it.

Her cell timer chimed.

"And now Mr. Ryan. It's time to check on you."

Ava slid over the duct-taped seats of her Explorer. Her internal jury remained undecided about Ryan's teen supervision. Until her mommy radar stopped chirping, she planned to make safety checks on Whit and Nate. Ryan would see right through her smoothie stop, but she didn't care. He'd screwed up once. She wasn't going to give him a repeat opportunity.

MAN, she hated it when she was wrong. How could a woman's steely resistance melt into gelatin in thirty short minutes? Ava froze behind Ryan's house, her fingers curling around the cardboard cup holder of three large smoothies. So much for her resolve to ignore Ryan's physical attraction, especially with the way sweat was snaking down his body and disappearing in his low-hanging jeans. Now she'd have a permanent image of his naked torso to haunt her dreams.

Whit looked up and held up a hand. Next time she needed to check on her boys, she'd call.

Determined to ignore the flutter in her belly, she marched to the edge of the short brown grass. "Working hard?"

Ryan grinned, once again transforming his somewhat attractive features into— Her mouth dried so fast her lips stuck to her teeth. She'd have to get over how his sudden smiles messed with her.

"Hey, you missed lunch." Darn his sexy voice.

She unglued her lips with her tongue and held up her offering. "Smoothie?"

Thank goodness for her sons. Within moments their tools hit the ground and they surrounded her.

"You must have read my mind," Nate said.

She handed him a cup. "Banana blueberry." Turning she handed the second cup to Whit. "Pineapple-orange."

Ignoring Ryan's intense gaze, she held out the third cup. "Strawberry-banana. That's Kyle's favorite. If you don't like it, I figured I could take it home."

While she tracked the flex of his arms and shoulders, he picked up a tan t-shirt and wiped the sweat from his face. Maybe she should take him home with the smoothie.

"You found the best drink shop in Sunberry. Gina's Eats and Treats serves awesome smoothies." He tossed the shirt over his shoulder. "I like them all."

His warm flesh brushed her fingers during the exchange. She straightened. No doubt, one interested blue and one brown gaze followed her movements like their lab followed a piece of jerky.

"Take ten." Ryan motioned her toward the house. "How's the patient?"

"Fine. According to the complaints from his nurse, he slept all morning."

While the boys settled at the patio table with their treats, he opened the back door for her to enter the house.

"Have a seat," he said. "I need a fresh shirt."

Excellent idea, for both of their sakes.

Uncomfortable alone in his home, Ava moved around the large open area. Although the brick ranch was constructed in the sixties, the room was large and open with a fireplace on one wall and a bank of windows facing the backyard. Unlike images of her bachelor-pad perception, Ryan maintained a tidy and comfortable home. The dark leather furniture shouted a masculine presence, but the family photos lining the mantle softened the decor.

In a silver frame, two teenaged girls and an elementary school-aged Ryan grinned at her from a backyard swing. His two older sisters, she guessed. Her gaze passed a youthful photo of Ryan's parents. She halted, and her breath stilled at the image in the small frame on the end.

"That was taken in Afghanistan." His deep voice carried from behind her.

With an unsteady grip, she replaced the photo of Ryan and Josh smiling in front of a Humvee. "He thought you were a good officer."

"Marines like him made me look good."

Based on the distance in his gaze and the softness of his tone, he'd omitted part of the story. *He lost Josh.* She swallowed. So much for forgiveness. However, the raw ache that accompanied memories of Josh had eased over time and so had her perceptions.

Ryan picked up the smoothie he'd left on the end table and sucked on the straw. The man had a luscious mouth. He was probably a good kisser. Heat singed her cheeks and she hoped a blush hadn't given her away. His Hawaiian shirt with huge red and blue flowers ruined her view of his bare chest. Worse, he'd washed away the bits of foliage that had clung to his forehead and cheeks, spoiling his rolled-in-the leaves look. More like rolled in the sheets. Heavens, her mind was an absolute mess.

Her heart thudded in her ears. She was a mother. Yes, and life was too short to let regret and bitterness taint it. Avoiding his alluring dark gaze, she stared at the ridiculous shirt. Her lips twitched. People often surprised her, but not as much as Ryan Murphy. Something about him made her yearn for a life shake up. Maybe she needed a life. Her own life. Not as a mother, but as a woman.

The hum of the air conditioner broke the silence. Tension tightened around her. She could almost hear the spin of his thoughts in the stillness. Her heart thumped harder in her chest. She sensed he had something to say, something important, something that might turn her stomach.

He stepped closer, the heat of his body invading her personal space. The scent of soap and man filled the air that had gotten a tad scarce in the past moments. The photo of Josh's big smile grounded her, dimmed Ryan's allure. Somewhat.

She lifted her gaze and released a breath. For once she wanted to turn loose, release her inhibitions, enjoy the rush of need filling her veins. But she'd have to continue to want for now.

"I made the right decision," she whispered, uncertain if she'd uttered the words for herself or Ryan.

"For your family," he said. "What about for you? Because it's going to happen. I thought so earlier. Now—" His gaze dropped to her lips and then returned. "Now, I'm sure of it."

She swallowed. So he disagreed. Men were always eager for something they couldn't have. Except he didn't fit the stereotype. He'd already proven that.

"What makes you so sure?"

"Because you're here." He cocked his head. "No matter

how much you deny it to me, to yourself, it's going to happen. We're going to happen. As for your boys, they'll come around."

"But I won't. We agreed." She hated the wobble in her voice as much as the doubt in her decision.

"You made a stance." His brows raised. "I didn't challenge you."

The sincere set to his chin and his clear unblinking gaze failed to trigger her nonsense alarm. Josh had been honest. Yeah, and Josh expected her to raise his sons. Not hook up with a man that might care for her but not understand boys. Josh would also accept the responsibility for what happened, not blame Ryan. She shifted. Josh wasn't here.

When Ryan's gaze returned to the photo, the energy charging the air vanished and her responsibilities settled against her shoulders. Outside, Whit and Nate moved across the yard, laughing together despite the heat and the work. But even if they learned to accept Ryan, his career remained an obstacle. Her chest seized accelerating her heartrate. In the future Ryan would return to another dangerous place in the world. Like Josh, he could die there. She could not expose her family to another loss.

She winced at the bite of her nails and released her fists. Ryan was studying her.

"So why are you so sure they'll change their minds?" *And I won't?* Because she wanted him to change her mind. To do something, say something to convince her they could be together.

He stepped forward as if her question had been the answer, had been yes. The minty smell of his soap filled her head. His size didn't intimidate her. Instead, a sense of safety, comfort, and heat swept over her. His magnetism pulled, tempted her. She resisted but didn't step back.

His fingers caught a tendril tickling her cheek. She hadn't

cleaned up before coming. Why should she? She wasn't looking for a man. She was checking on her sons.

His fingers lingered, ran along her jaw, behind her neck. An involuntary shiver raced along her spine but more from the look in his eye than his touch.

"I'm working on that." He closed the distance between them, his voice soft, beckoning. "I'm also working on why being around you messes with my head. Makes me want to ignore the rules."

"Marines adhere to the code of honor," she whispered. And to their call of duty.

"When you look at me like that, moisten your lips, curl your hands in my shirt, the code evaporates."

She glanced at her traitorous fingers knotting the flowery fabric but didn't relax her grip.

"I need to kiss you." His breath, scented with strawberries, fanned her cheek. "Tell me it's okay. Tell me you want this, if only for this moment."

No! "Just once."

He touched her lips with his, the lightest of kisses. She sighed against him and the hint of need and want fired deep in her belly. She wanted him. Wanted his flesh against hers. Wanted his ragged breathing blending with hers. Wanted to soar with him without thought.

When he released her, a breath whispered past her lips.

"Don't deny you felt something." His ragged tone tore through her.

"I won't," she whispered. "But I'm not free to engage in a fast affair." She held his gaze. He deserved her honesty. "But that doesn't mean I don't think about you. Think about what happens when you look at me. When you kiss me."

Her admission should've embarrassed her. Instead, it fueled the images locked in her mind, gave her strength. His expression hardened and he tucked his chin like he expected a punch. He was struggling the same as she was. What he wanted also broke his rules. Made him feel out of control. Worse, she wanted him—out of control. And *that* wasn't going to happen.

"I can't get involved without considering the impact on my family."

Ryan raked a hand through his hair. "I was thinking about dinner."

The situation was funny and sad.

"I was thinking about *after* dinner." She pressed her palms against his hard chest and pushed. He stepped back, but his gaze sparked with sexual interest.

"It's unstoppable." He shook his head. "I've tried. Even convinced myself once or twice. But then you say something, or do something, or look a certain way, and all my discipline —" He snapped his fingers. "Boom. Gone. And I think about holding you, touching you—"

"That's ... honest, *Major.*" She'd added his title to keep her mind right. Because she'd never been turned on by a man's words. At least not in a long time. But she could give honesty as good as she could take it. "Just like I don't question the desire to feel your arms around me."

And if he didn't cool the hooded sexy look, she might initiate that embrace. "However, I must act on the greater good of my family. And you—" She jabbed him in the chest with her index finger. "Must act on your code of honor." She jabbed again. "We're going to maintain a friendship. You're going to help me with my place. And for now, that's all."

He turned and picked up his drink as if her words hadn't cooled his ardor. Her gaze fell to his lips pursed around the straw. She liked his mouth. Liked the way it moved against hers. Maybe she'd find out if the rest of him created the same tingling inside her, someday.

No doubt, he'd suffer a brain freeze if he didn't quit

pulling on the straw. When he winced, she bit her lip to stifle a smile. *Nothing like being right.*

"Glad we got that out of the way." He massaged his right temple. "But your sons will come around. And sooner than you think. I work with Marines every day."

"They lost their father. They don't want a replacement."

His eyes widened a few centimeters. But she'd learned long ago how to throw men off-balance. The gift gave her an edge and compensated for what she lacked in size.

He sobered. "Someone hurt you."

Okay, she'd give him that one. "My mother divorced when I was five. My stepfather was a decent man. He didn't abuse me or anything. But I was invisible."

"And your biological father?"

"The last time I saw him was sometime before my sixth birthday. He was supposed to come. He didn't."

"And your mother?"

Outside, shafts of sunlight highlighted the gold in Whit's hair and fired streaks of red in Nate's dark locks. "Mom wanted a man to love her. Now, I understand why."

He did that nodding thing again. She still hadn't figured out if the gesture was a yes or acknowledgement that he was thinking and considering what he'd heard. She didn't expect to get close enough to work that out. But her recent expectations had missed the mark, big time.

When she moved toward the front door, he followed.

"If it's late when we finish." His gaze drifted from her eyes to her lips and back. "I'll drive them home."

The urge to disagree curled her fingers, but she didn't press. She'd said enough, felt enough for one day.

"Perfect." She narrowed her gaze on him to let him know she hadn't missed his infringement. "Until that time, keep them safe."

But who was going to keep her safe from him?

CHAPTER EIGHT

At three that afternoon, Ryan rested his scythe. "Take a break."

The two teens turned his way, put down their tools, and headed toward the house, wiping sweaty faces with wet t-shirts. The Robey boys carried traits from Ava and his Sergeant. Ava left her genetic stamp, complete with dark hair and eyes, on all but the middle boy. His sandy hair and blue eyes came from Sergeant Robey.

The whisper of a welcome breeze lifted wet hair at Ryan's temples. Robey had been a good Marine and a good man. No doubt he'd been a good father. Too bad he didn't get the chance to finish the job. One miscalculation and boom, game over.

Ryan held the hose over the back of his neck. Twigs, grass, and dirt sluiced down his arms and cooled his flesh. Beside him, Nate scrubbed his dark hair with dirt-crusted hands.

"It's not cold, but it feels good." Ryan passed the hose to him. "I'll get towels."

By the time Nate and Whit had washed off a layer of

sweat and foliage debris, Ryan returned with clean towels and two of his old t-shirts.

"They might fit big, but they're clean and dry."

Whit dropped his dirty t-shirt on the concrete near the entrance to the house. Tall and lean, his baggy jeans hanging low on his hips, the kid stood about three inches taller than his broader little brother.

Ryan extracted three drinks from the cooler and set them on the picnic table. Robey would've been proud of the way his sons turned out—*if* Ava could steer them clear of trouble. That's where he came in. Although too late for football, his friend Coach Cox could draft the Robey boys on the soccer or basketball team. Chuck was always complaining about the low turnout and sports kept boys out of trouble.

Ryan uncapped a drink. "It's not supposed to be this hot in November."

Whit grabbed opposite ends of a towel and seesawed his back. "Mom says there's no *supposed to* in life. It just is."

Nate ignored the towel and tore into the chips. "My stomach thinks my throat's been cut."

Stunned, Ryan raised his palms. "My tongue is glued to the roof of my mouth. How can you eat without drinking first?"

Whit uncapped his drink. "He's an eating machine."

"Your stomach isn't a bottomless pit. It's a black hole." Ryan drained the second third of his bottle. "Your food bill probably exceeds the National debt."

When Nate stopped chewing, Ryan waved him on. "Eat. There's more where that came from." He tapped his phone. "I figure we can get in another two hours before quitting."

Whit gulped half of his drink and wiped his mouth on the back of his forearm. "We should make it through the heavy stuff by then, if you can keep up."

Ryan lifted his bottle. "Getting cocky on me?"

Whit shrugged again, but the left side of his mouth twitched upward. "Just saying you were behind."

True, but Ryan wasn't ready to concede. "You swing a mean scythe."

Only the sound of crunching broke the silence. He hid a smile. Nothing like hard work to build a kid's appetite and loosen their tongues.

He wiped his forehead with his arm. "How do you like living in Sunberry?"

"It's okay," Whit said around a mouthful of chips.

"Kyle hates it," Nate said.

"Kyle hates everything," Whit added.

Ryan emptied the remains of one bag of chips on a plate. "How about your mom?"

Whit studied him.

So what's messing with you? Ryan polished off his Gatorade and opened a second bottle.

"Mom always loved Gran's place. It needed more work than she thought." Whit wiped his mouth and poured another large mound of chips on his plate.

"We're going to open a Robey business," Nate said.

Whit glared at his brother. "Family business is private. Only Robeys work on it and talk about it."

Whoa, touchy topic. Ryan lobbed the wadded chip bag into the garbage. "I admire a man who knows the importance of discretion."

Just because he agreed to honor Ava's instructions, didn't mean he'd muzzle his curiosity. Besides, it didn't make sense to keep a business secret. Word of mouth was a powerful marketing technique. Personal references made a successful business.

Nate picked through the remaining chips on his napkin. "Mom's into recycling."

The kid glanced at his big brother and got the okay. The

boys weren't immune to trouble, but they also respected Ava's wishes, admirable trait for teenagers. Most of the kids were so oppositional to authority they'd engage into all sorts of trouble. He washed down the salty snack with a long drink. He'd been wrong to classify the Robey boys as delinquents.

Whit arced his empty beverage bottle into the air. It thudded into the center of the trash can beside the door. "She doesn't throw things out because they aren't perfect."

Like him. Ryan pulled another Gatorade from the cooler and handed one to each teen.

"Is she still going to do it?"

Nate shrugged.

Whit focused on wadding his napkin. After a few moments, he looked up. "Mom wanted to be her own boss. After Grandma died..." He shrugged.

Ryan covered a belch with his hand. Nothing worse than having your dreams go up in smoke. If the board passed him, he was through. No more Corp. No more job he loved. No more chances to turn things around at the base. Although he guzzled another drink, the liquid didn't relieve the constriction in his neck.

The Corps was his family, a community of people who gave him purpose and a common connection. He loved his biological family, but they came with the Murphy package. His Corps community was developed by a shared history often created under fire. Life for him wouldn't work without his military family. That's why he understood Ava's stubbornness to build more shared history with her sons.

He blinked. The hum of insects sharpened the silence.

"We don't have to discuss the *Robey business.* I'd like to come up with a way to help your Mom. I don't care what it is. It could be personal, something around the farm."

Silence.

Ryan stood. "I've got a bag of Oreos. Are you interested?"

"Sure," Nate said.

Whit elbowed his brother.

Nate rubbed his side. "I'm hungry. We've been working all day."

Whit shot him a *whatever* look.

In the kitchen, Ryan grabbed the family-sized package. Nate had a point. No doubt hunger drove Whit just as hard. He practiced more discipline when it came to following his mother's rules. The kid also didn't refuse food. The boys held a wealth of information about the family's needs. A smart man always mined intel opportunities.

Outside, Ryan opened and placed the snack in the middle of the table. "Have you signed up for sports? I'm sure Sunberry could use players with your size."

Nothing but chewing. So much for easing back into the conversation.

"So if you could do anything to help your mom, what would it be?"

Whit studied the Gatorade bottle. "Make good grades."

"Stay out of trouble," Nate offered.

Ryan stifled a groan. "I'm sure she'd appreciate your efforts. So, any thoughts about a special project? Something around the farm your Mom wants to do but hasn't gotten to it." More like couldn't afford to do, but he needed to keep the teens talking not close them down.

Nate stuffed three cookies into his mouth.

Whit wrapped four cookies in a napkin. "I thought I'd save some for later."

The kid practiced tight judgement for a teen. Ryan waited. Instinct told him the teen with his dad's looks would reveal the most about the family.

Whit glanced at Ryan. "Grandma and Mom made a list."

"That's what I did when I moved here." Ryan waved a hand at the lot. "Clearing the back was the last thing on it."

"No shit," Nate said. "I would've scratched it off."

"Good point." Ryan suppressed a grin. The young always had a refreshing and honest perspective. "So what's on your Mom's list?"

Whit studied him with the wisdom of a much older guy. On first meeting, he'd pegged Kyle with the highest IQ. However, Whit came in a close second. The boy was sharp and discreet. Probably could keep his mouth shut in extreme circumstances.

"Why do you want to know?"

Ryan sucked in his cheeks. The kid was also suspicious. *When in doubt, go with the truth.* "Marines take care of one another. That means families too."

Whit's eyes narrowed but not with the same anger in his older brother's gaze. With this kid, it was more wariness. "You were the one at the door. The day they told us about Dad."

Shit. He was hoping the boys didn't remember. Hell, he didn't want to remember one of the worst days of his life. Images of firefights exploded in his head. Although he hadn't been there when his Sergeant needed him most, he'd seen enough combat to fill in the blanks. Sweat snaked down his hairline. A gnat buzzed near his ear. But no munching. Whit and Nate stared at him.

"It was me." He cringed at the rusty sound of his voice.

"So you aren't hitting on her?" Whit said.

Ryan grunted. Talk about a sucker punch. But he wasn't going to lie. "She's an attractive woman. But your dad always had my back. I'd like to return the service."

Whit studied him with narrowed eyes and an odd quirk to his mouth. "The barn roof."

"Do you boys know anything about roofing?"

Whit squared his shoulders. "Didn't know anything about floors until a few weeks ago."

"Too bad Kyle didn't watch a video on the proper use of chainsaws." Ryan snapped his jaw shut.

Whit jerked to his feet. "With Kyle laid up and us here, Mom's probably working alone."

Nate stopped chewing, his gaze tracking to his big brother. He shoved the cookie package to the center of the table. "We better get back to work."

"I know you don't have to help. That wasn't part of the deal." Whit capped the empty bottle and tossed it into the trash receptacle. "But thanks."

Ryan could've handled a punch better than the kid's softly spoken words. "When you get home tonight, tell her we finished."

Whit shook his head. "She won't believe us."

"She'll check." Nate nodded. "Mom always checks."

"That's one of the reasons she came over," Whit said.

"Hell." Ryan tossed each boy another drink to take with them. "She makes it hard to help her out. This isn't a handout. Marines take care of Marines. End of story."

"Mom's stubborn," Whit admitted.

"Here's the plan."

Both boys halted, and their gazes held his. He had them. Now he had to keep them.

"I'll get some Marines to help me with the barn roof. If something more urgent comes up, let me know. You two are my eyes and ears."

They didn't look convinced, but they didn't say no. "As far as your Mom's concerned, we finish tomorrow. That will clear your time to help her. Tell her tonight, so she gets used to the idea."

Nate looked at his older brother. Whit shrugged. "It could work."

"We'll work until dark." Ryan retrieved the scythe. "I'll drive you home."

A coded look passed between the two boys. They might know Ava, but they didn't know him, and neither did their mother. She wasn't going to scare him off because she came with a ready-made family. He liked her boys. With finesse he figured he could get them to see things his way. Ava Robey better watch her flank because this Marine wasn't turning back.

WHEN RYAN WHEELED onto Ava's rutted drive the next morning, his headlight beam cut through the predawn gloom. He hoped the boys would be late so he'd have time for a cup of coffee with Ava on that swing with the sunrise painting the sky. He grunted. Next, he'd be spouting poetry.

Today, he needed to convince Ava the yard work was almost done, and then bust his chops to finish it before tomorrow evening. He'd already lost a day in the competition. Wouldn't do him any good to fix Ava and have Schmidt blow up.

He stopped in front of her house and cut the engine. Although dim, a light shown through the front window. Kitchen light, he guessed. Maybe that cup of coffee wasn't so far off. A squirrel barked a back-off warning from the live oak guarding the old house. He moved forward.

The front door creaked, and Whit stepped outside. Disappointment forced Ryan's breath out in a huff.

"Morning Major," Whit said. "Can you give us five minutes? Mom has coffee."

Ava, dressed in a pair of jeans and a faded plaid shirt, stepped onto the porch. No bandana bound her head. Rich dark hair framed her face and brushed her shoulders. Why'd she bind it up? Hair like that needed to be free so a man could run his fingers through it, smooth it back to expose the creamy skin of her throat.

She held out a cup, its contents billowing steam in the early morning chill. "Nate and Whit are finishing up kitchen detail."

Ryan dropped his gaze to meet hers. She'd been watching, but at least she caught him staring at her hair and not somewhere else. Her chin lifted along with her right brow.

His heart accelerated. "Thanks. My morning just improved."

She settled onto the swing. "The boys said you're hoping to finish today."

"That's our plan."

An errant tendril caught the light. He liked this side of her. And he better concentrate on his words instead of the images in his head. Figuring she'd fuss if he cozied up beside her, he sat on the opposite side of the swing. Her narrowed gaze sounded an alarm in his head.

"They're faster than I anticipated." He measured his explanation. "You don't often find that quality with young men. You've raised them right."

He'd never thought much about a woman's eyebrows, but Ava changed all of that. His brows were heavy and sometimes wild, keeping some of the sweat out of his eyes. Ava's seemed to talk. His compliment had sent the right one upward, causing all kinds of sensations in places that didn't need to be reacting, at least not now with too many eyes on them.

"Thank you. I try." But her snicker indicated a secret.

"No ma'am. You do more than try. You succeed." And she was sure succeeding with him. Just not in the way he'd imagined.

"And you're still trying to change my mind."

He winked. But if she blushed, the dim morning light hid it.

"Marine on a mission." He rocked the swing. "This is nice."

It would be nicer with her head on his shoulder. Her dark hair tickling his chin. Her woman's scent filling his head.

"So I'm supposed to believe you finished clearing at least half-way to your property line?"

Her tone held a bite blended with humor. Ava kept a man on the ready. He liked that about her. Liked that he had a hot cup of joe to keep from grinning. "Sounds accurate."

"Which means you cleared twice as much land yesterday afternoon as you did in the morning."

She'd moved from suspicious to incredulous. The woman was perceptive. He wanted to laugh. Everything about her was fun, surprising, sexy.

He turned to her, a major mistake. If he caved into messed hair and sleep-swollen features, he'd lose his edge. Crap, she was already studying him.

He straightened. "Accurate assessment. Whit and I had a competition in the afternoon. He forced me to up my game."

"*Forced* you? Right."

"Just a friendly gentleman's competition." Man, she wasn't giving up. "I couldn't let a young buck show me up."

"Of course not." Her features softened. "I'm still checking."

He lifted his mug to her. "Didn't figure any other way."

Her luminous eyes peered over the rim of her mug. "I thought you said you had something else you needed to do."

Way to ruin a good encounter. "I do. But it's on hold until Tuesday."

It sucked, but he couldn't accelerate the ceiling supply delivery. He'd have to bust it after work this week. He'd bust Schmidt if he hadn't made an appointment.

The swing shifted. Holy crap, she'd moved closer. The rosy glow from the sunrise highlighted her shadowed face. He stifled the urge to lean closer, confide his problem with Schmidt.

"That's probably driving a man like you crazy."

He straightened. *She didn't know the half of it.* "Nobody likes a delay. So was that a compliment or a criticism?"

"How about accurate? You're decisive. Man of action. A fixer. And something out of your control is making you wait." She smiled. "Like me."

"Don't break your arm patting your back." But he was thankful she'd eased her charge.

She was right about him. Hell, he was beginning to think she was right most of the time, but just when he was wrong. And he tried to avoid that when possible.

She blew on her knuckles and then rubbed them across her chest. "I must revel in my successes. One never knows when the next one will come along."

Male voices and boards creaking warned of the boys' approach.

He pushed to his feet. "I'm due for a success too." *With her.*

When she stood beside him, the old swing creaked, sending a flash of screeching bedsprings through his head. Double-timing it, he hustled down the ancient porch steps.

She followed him to the car. "Since you're driving them in, I'll pick them up. Besides," she added with a hint of skepticism. "I'd like to see the finished product."

Nate said she'd check on their progress. The kid knew his mother.

"It will take us until dark to finish." Ryan froze to maintain his cover. "I'll feed them dinner before I bring them home."

The old stubbornness returned to her narrowed eyes. "We agreed to lunch."

He opened the car door, but she didn't back off. Nate and Whit climbed in the back. Avoiding her gaze, he adjusted his seat, checked his back pocket, and then slid behind the wheel. After adjusting the rearview to check the boys' stoic faces, he met her narrowed-eye expression.

"We didn't consider working this late." He stuck to the facts, nice and easy. "I'd like to finish before the weather changes."

She'd moved in front of the door so he couldn't close it. "It's going to be another hot day. I'll bring smoothies."

"I thought you had a project." Steady. No head bobbing. "I have a cooler of Gatorade. I was thinking about a celebration Monday evening. I'll put steaks on the grill and Nate and Whit can show off their work."

From the sudden silence inside the vehicle, his offer had the boys' undivided attention. No doubt, Nate was already salivating over the prospect of a thick steak. Whit was interested in the interplay between Ryan and his mother.

When Ava lifted her chin, Ryan held his breath.

"Should I bring something?"

He gripped the steering wheel so he didn't grab her cheeks between his hands and give her a big sloppy kiss. That would get him nowhere, so he gave her his biggest smile. "One of your home-made pies would be appreciated."

Her eyebrow raised. "Any certain kind?"

His mind reverted to one track, and it was one hundred clicks from dessert. "I like them all." Especially if she made it.

The hint of her smile tempted him, but he kept his features straight. With three sons she'd probably aced patience.

"Don't be late," she said. "Tomorrow's a school day."

"We're burning daylight," Whit said.

"That's my line," Ryan muttered.

"And Ryan—"

Her voice was low and tentative like something was up.

"That project you mentioned." She pressed her palm to

his forearm. "You ... you looked like it was important. Let me know if I can help."

Go figure. With all the worries on her plate, she was asking about him. "Thanks." His voice sounded hoarse so he cleared his throat. "I'm okay for now."

His SUV engine hummed to life. When he checked the rearview again, Whit was tracking him like a sniper. *Nope*. Ryan wasn't close to okay and the kid picked up on it. The boys would have to get over it like he had. Their prickly, independent mother had slipped through his defense line and targeted his heart and soul. And he was liking every minute of it.

CHAPTER NINE

STIFF AND SORE FROM HER FIRST DAY AT THE WORK SITE, Ava pushed from bed early Sunday morning. The sun had begun a slow march to the sky and split the clouds with coral and gold hues. After fixing a cup of coffee she pulled the sash on her tattered terry robe and moved to the back porch.

While Toby bounded out the back, nose to the ground, she settled into Gran's old rocker and breathed in the scent of pine hinted with brine. Although weathered, she loved Gran's farm and the memories the buildings held. The hot coffee warmed her insides much faster than the sun crawling over the eastern horizon warmed the porch.

She snuggled deeper into her robe. Summer's hold on North Carolina was slipping into fall the same as her dream to open the shop before the holidays. Especially after yesterday's cleaning revelations. The College Street property wasn't a commercial site. It was a garbage dump.

When Kyle's shadow passed the kitchen window, she pushed to her feet.

Ava eased the backdoor closed. "How's the leg?"

"It doesn't burn as bad as yesterday." He filled a bowl with flakes and added milk. "I'll go with you today."

Ava washed out her cup and set it on a towel to dry. "Thanks, but the place is filthy. If your wound gets infected, it will take twice as long to heal."

"There's nothing wrong with my arms. I can paint."

Why couldn't he just talk? With Kyle, everything seemed to be an argument. He was her negotiator, never satisfied with a simple yes or no. But this snarly tone was starting to get old. Her shoulders sagged. He hadn't accepted Josh's loss or maybe the real problem was forgiveness. It seemed like he blamed Josh for not living, not coming home. Worse, she didn't know how to help him.

She touched his shoulder to find a corded muscle had replaced his baby pudge. "Kyle, I'm your mother, not the enemy."

Something flickered in his dark eyes. Regret? She couldn't tell, but it was a start.

"Dad wouldn't want you to go alone."

OMG, was his tough shell breaking? The breath she'd been holding whooshed from her lungs. "He wouldn't want you to reinjure your leg. I'll be fine. I'm cleaning out the junk so we can start the real work."

Kyle smacked the table with his fist. "This really pisses me off! I was trying to speed up the work so we could finish and help you."

She knelt beside him and reached for his fist. He pulled away, but she captured it and her love-gorged heart threatened to pound an opening through her ribs.

"Thank you. But never minimize what you give to me. You, Whit, Nate, and Hope help me every day. You're the reason I'm here. The reason I dream of a family business."

"A lot of good I do you," he muttered.

He didn't pull away from her embrace.

"Aah, but that's where you're wrong." She yearned to nuzzle his cheek with its soft patches of whiskers, but kissed his head instead. "We have six weeks and there *will* be a Robey business."

He pushed his too long dark hair away from his face. "Not unless we start helping."

"Since when do Robeys give up?"

Although he rolled his eyes, a hint of a smile tugged at the corner of his mouth. Praise be. Her wonderful first-born still occupied that lean body. She'd had her doubts over the past few months, but he was starting to emerge, if one paid close attention.

"Rest up and keep Hope occupied. That's a big help. I'll remove the last of the trash and start painting tomorrow while you're in school."

He gulped his juice. "We can all help tomorrow evening."

"After homework is done."

"What about a bathroom?" He spooned a huge mouthful of cereal, chewed, and swallowed. "Give me a roller on a pole. I can sit down and paint. Hope can be my gopher."

"You're good Kyle Robey." She shook her head. "I'll give you that. I think law is your calling."

"I'm going to med school." He straightened in his chair. "But I'm not just good. I'm right."

"And arrogant." She softened her words with a smile.

"Confident," Kyle corrected. "I can knock out a bathroom with no risk to my leg."

Mercy, she was such a sucker for the charm. "You promise to stay seated?"

When he held up three fingers, an image of her cub scout sent hot tears stinging her eyes.

"Maybe for half a day." She was such a soft touch and he knew it.

Kyle shrugged. "We can assess at lunch."

Triumph laced his smirk.

"If you show a hint of fatigue, I'm packing you up and hauling you home."

He held out his fist. Mothers needed to be strong. She bumped his knuckles with hers, a smile filling her heart at the same time it lifted her lips. It had been such a long time since she'd connected with him, really connected.

"I better wake Hope."

"And Mom?"

The serious pitch of his voice lifted the hair on her neck. When she turned a man residing in her teenaged son met her gaze. "Whit and Nate think Ryan is a good guy."

"But not you?" she questioned.

"He's okay, I guess. But we don't need him. We're doing okay, just us."

So that's what was eating at her oldest. "We've had our share of hard knocks, but it's okay to accept help from friends and neighbors."

"Whit thinks they may finish today."

Toby moved by her side, his big, silky head solid and loving beneath her fingers. "Ryan mentioned that. Which seems odd. I saw the infamous *jungle.* I estimated it would take a bulldozer two days to clean out the brush and vines."

"If Ryan hadn't pitched in, it probably would have. He helped all day long."

Ryan had also driven her boys home in his SUV.

Something flickered in Kyle's expression. Heavens, she was getting paranoid in her old age. Or smart.

"He's got the hots for you."

Saliva leaked into her windpipe. Which was not the cool confident way to handle Kyle's remark. "I don't—" she coughed again. "I didn't expect that."

"I've seen the way he looks at you. Whit gets the same sappy look every time he's around Talley."

"It's different for adults." Which her perceptive son was not buying. She was so unprepared for this discussion.

"I'm not a little kid. When it comes to women, neither are my brothers."

Women? Where was she while her son was growing up? "I better dust off my protection talk."

"I got it Mom." He held up his palms. "I'm not talking about girls. I'm talking about Robey's Rewards. We messed up fighting and I made it worse with my accident. It was stupid. I admit it. It won't happen again."

He was too young to be the man of the house. Acid simmered in her gut. Josh shouldn't have died. It wasn't fair to leave three boys fatherless and rob them of their childhood. Blinking hard, she turned her face aside and squeezed his lean shoulder.

"We all make mistakes. That's how we learn. But let me be clear: nothing you do will stop me from loving you."

This time, she didn't hide her tears. Her son deserved honesty and so did she. Kyle's attitude had changed so maybe she could accept Ryan's invitation to date. Ava pulled her bathrobe tighter. It was too soon to take a chance.

Kyle had risked his life to help her build Robey's Rewards. To be the Robey man of the house. To assume a role he was unprepared to fill. Her son needed understanding, not an adult competitor. That meant a future, even a casual dating prospect, was off the table. Priority one: family. Priority two: business. No number three existed. No man occupied the Robey plan.

SAYING her plan didn't include Ryan and living it continued to haunt her at four-thirty on Monday. Even if she were childless, which she wasn't, Ryan wasn't a good match for her. The Corps had hard-wired serve and protect in his DNA. Which knotted her panties every time the thought passed through her brain. He could talk the talk, but she did *not* believe he'd change, ever.

But darn the man, he also listened to her and valued her opinion. Plus, the physical thing. She flipped the blinker. Around him she didn't recognize herself. It was like living with a stranger. And she was kicking that stranger to the curb.

So why was she taking her family to Ryan's for dinner? She inched through the school pickup traffic. A woman with four children took risks. With Ryan she might as well step from a cliff blindfolded and hope for a net.

Five minutes after the school doors opened with an exodus of kids, her sons appeared with a pretty girl chatting among them.

Whit opened the back door. "Can we give Talley a ride? She lives next door to the Major."

Ava ignored the lovesick look on Whit's face. "As long as it's okay with her parents. But I want to stop at the job site before we head that way."

Ava ignored the groans from the backseat. "Hey, I wanted to show you my achievements too. Painting starts tomorrow."

"Aah no," Kyle said. "Painting started yesterday. One of the baths has a coat of paint."

"Mom's okay with the change," Talley said.

Nate waved from the backseat. "I'm starving."

Of course he was. "Suck it up." Ava put the Explorer in gear. "Besides, you need to see what's ahead every evening this week and the weekend."

"Mom," Kyle said. "We know what lies ahead."

"Do you think I could try out for a team this year?" Whit asked. "Ryan hooked me up with Coach Cox. He needs guys for basketball."

Ava's shoulders sagged against the torn seat back. Her

sons deserved fun and to be included in activities. Instead, they were forced to help her.

"I'm sure we could work around your schedule. Kyle, Nate are you interested in sports?"

Nate's gaze appeared in the rearview. "Sure. I've thought about it."

"Kyle?"

Although he didn't respond, she guessed he harbored the same desire. The Explorer squeaked and groaned with the turn into the parking lot behind the College Street property. She wheeled into the expansive asphalt, avoiding a pothole large enough to hide a child. The rear entrance offered ample parking and ease of entry, a bonus for custom-painted furniture sales. Robey's Rewards also required heavy foot traffic. The kind generated by the Opera House. People who appreciated live theatre often appreciated hand-painted scenes on quality wood pieces.

With her work over the past few days, her dream had moved closer. She shifted into park. "They picked up the garbage today!"

"Mom gets pumped about the garbage truck," Whit said.

Kyle bumped his shoulder against his door to get it to release. "We latch the screen at home so she doesn't run into the road on garbage day."

"Stop." Ava laughed, happy her sons had a friend. Happy to share their fun.

At the back door to the property, Ava inserted the key. It didn't turn. Holding her breath, she jiggled the lock.

"It's tight, but it works."

Although her sons remained silent, their skepticism darted her back like daggers. Gritting her teeth, she shook the door handle and the tumblers fell into place. With a flick of her arm, she muscled the back door open and let them precede her inside.

"Well?"

Her breath hung in her chest. They had to notice. Two days ago, junk obscured the walls.

Talley moved through the kitchen to the large front room and turned. "I bet this was an awesome house in its day. Too bad Mr. Butler doesn't rent to college kids. Wouldn't it be cool to share it with three people? You could walk to class from here."

"Big rooms to paint," Nate muttered.

"Mrs. Robey, you should talk to Mom and Major Murphy. When we painted our house, they hosted a paint party. A bunch of Marines came over and painted the house in a day. We had pizza and beer. It was cool. I met a bunch of new friends."

Whit shot Ava a sad-eyed look that hurt her chest.

"You don't understand the Robey way." Kyle limped to the middle of the room. "This place is a steppingstone to the place Mom wants to lease on Main Street. It's ours. Just Robeys."

Talley shrugged. "Whatever. Just a thought."

"Come on." Ava forced a smile, hoping her voice would follow the lead. It didn't. "Check out the back rooms. Kyle painted one coat on the bathroom yesterday."

But she couldn't revive the carefree mood. At least not for her and Kyle. He'd sounded so cynical and closed off. Did he get that from her? By the time they picked up Hope, gas and wandered through the hardware store, they were due for the cookout. Ava took the longest route to Ryan's address. When she approached the turn, she accelerated. Four heads bobbed in her rearview mirror. The natives in the back would complain. She decreased the pressure on the accelerator and bumped the turn signal.

Her skin started prickling the minute she stopped in Ryan's drive. This was a bad idea. But she'd have an all-out war on her hands if she locked the doors and drove her hungry brood home. It was a cookout with four adolescents and Hope. Her fingers contracted around the steering wheel. She shouldn't be here. Ryan checked too many boxes on her Man Must-Have list.

"Ugh." Since when did she have a list for a man?

Behind her the kids scrambled out in their usual chaotic manner. Waves of pinpricks marched along her arms. *Breathe in. Breathe out.*

She switched off the key. Her Explorer backfired and shuddered to a halt.

Ryan opened her car door. "Sounds like your ride needs to visit Quinn's."

Her heart almost stopped.

"Didn't mean to startle you," he said.

He probably didn't mean to turn her life upside down, but he had. Thank goodness he didn't grin and show off his dimples or wink. His frown made his features hard and intense, but darned him, he still looked sexy. And now he was worried about her old car.

She patted the red cracked dash with a shaky hand. "Goldie is like an assertive woman. She always has to get in the final word."

Although Ryan's brow furrowed, he had the good sense to remain mute, *if* she didn't count the sudden widening of his eyes.

"Goldie is a perfect name for a red car."

She wouldn't dignify his comment with a response.

While her sons followed Talley next door to drop off her bookbag, Ryan led her through the house to the screened-in back porch. A blue-plaid tablecloth and matching place settings for seven covered the large table.

"Wow!" She touched the pressed cotton. "I'm impressed."

"Don't be."

His breath whispered along her neck and a shiver of excitement ricocheted down her spine. Compared to her three rowdy young men, Ryan moved like a cat, almost soundless.

"Mom drops off stuff so she can check up on me." He opened the backdoor for her. "Besides, the tablecloth saved me from scrubbing the table."

In the backyard the foursome emerged from next door and walked toward Ryan's decimated jungle. Ava sobered. With her handsome host and the party atmosphere, she'd forgotten the primary purpose of her visit.

Ryan opened the backdoor. "Time for the inspection. Nate and Whit are proud of the work."

Ava's mom-antennae wiggled like they did when her sons were trying to pull something over on her. The early completion was weird. Everything about Ryan shouted efficiency, planning. Yet, he'd missed the work projection by two days. Plus, she'd seen his so-called jungle and worried if her sons could complete the job in four days.

She'd been specific about the work exchange and her ethics. A mother couldn't just talk the talk. She had to demonstrate those principles to her fatherless boys.

At the perimeter of the site, a small yellow flag waved in the light breeze. Although the brown mowed lawn gave way to uneven ground, the vegetation had been cropped close to the soil. To the right a large black mark scorched the earth and the scent of charred vegetation hung in the air.

Ryan's gaze captured hers. "I burned it today. Perfect time with last night's rain."

First, he filled in for Kyle and then he'd finished the work while her sons were in school. None of those things were in their agreement. Her boys hadn't paid their debt. He'd waived it like she was a charity case.

Heat creeped up her neck. Oh, she knew this drill. Poor

Widow Robey needed a man to take care of her and her family. She didn't want his pity.

Talley's laughter chimed in the silence followed by the low chuckles of the boys. Ava's shoulders dropped. She should've checked her broom at the door. Although she didn't want Ryan obligated to her, he had done nothing but offer help and support. He deserved a response, deserved a thank-you not a complaint.

Ryan glanced at her, a tentative grin on his face. Her lips twitched. She couldn't help it. He looked like Toby hoping for a scratch behind his ears. Still, she'd address the issue later in private. She didn't want the man to get too confident.

"I'm never getting in the landscaping business," Whit muttered.

And she was never getting in Ryan's bed. Ava hurried to catch up with the group and put distance between Ryan and her hormones. Too bad the short walk around Ryan's so-called razed jungle didn't quiet her traitorous body.

"Is there something I can do?" Ava said ten minutes later.

Ryan forked marbled sirloins onto the grill. "Relax. Everything's ready. I bought salad in the bag. Hope that's okay."

"It's lovely." She sat in the cushioned chair. Nothing wrong with loosening up for one evening. And it wasn't like she was alone with the man. Leaning against the headrest, she inhaled the intoxicating scent of seasoned beef and charcoal.

Ryan handed her a plush blanket. "It's getting chilly."

Doomed. She was doomed. But it was such a treat to let someone else cook for a change. Let someone wait on her. Just not take care of her.

He opened the lid to the grill. "How's your project coming along?"

"Excellent." She might be behind schedule, but she made great headway. "I'll start painting tomorrow."

The hairs along her forearms lifted. Something was wrong with Ryan.

He flipped the steaks, and then waited for the steam to subside before closing the lid again. When he turned to her, the creases bracketing his mouth seemed deeper.

"Is something wrong?"

"A Marine is having trouble. Bad tour."

She gripped the armrests. Bad tour nothing. Men always looked away when they were omitting details. Which made sense. Ryan, always the protector, considered people around him, shielding them from pain and disappointment. The man really was a saint.

"I'm sorry." She resisted the urge to touch him, absorb the worry lining his brow. "That happened to Josh a couple of times. Is he getting help?"

He repositioned the steaks he'd turned, his glance rotating to her, to the kids, and then back to the grill. Her boys did the same nervous glance when something bad had happened and they didn't know how to tell her. And if he were anything like her boys, he'd speak his peace in his own time.

Ryan continued to fuss over the meat. After a few minutes he said, "He's old school Marine. You know the type, tough guy. Can muscle through anything."

But from the straight set of Ryan's lips and the tenor of his voice, she guessed the Marine's latest wasn't the usual *anything*.

"Deployment is hard on Marines and their families. I couldn't wait for Josh to come home." The not-so-good times filled her mind. "Then, he'd arrive, and he was ...different. The Corps warns wives about symptoms of PTSD, but it's so much more. The same man who left isn't always the man who comes home."

He nodded, a distant look in his gaze. "I think he and his

family are trying to manage the changes. He's scheduled to retire soon. I'm not sure if the impending change will help or exacerbate his situation."

A high-pitched laugh cut through her sons' chatter. At the edge of the yard, the teens clustered. While Whit remained closest to Talley's side, Nate and Kyle crowded near. Hope always managed to worm into the middle. All wore smiles. Ava released an easy breath. Talley's presence softened the lines between her three sons.

"Talley's had a rough go." Ryan lowered his voice again. "Bryce and Michelle are career Marines. They try to create a family, but it's still tough."

"Is that why you've stayed single?"

"Developing a relationship and a career has its challenges." His grimace looked more like a funny face. "Especially when you have to relocate every few years."

"I followed Josh to many locations, but we were always happy because we had one another," she said. "Family makes the home, not the place."

When he smiled, butterflies filled her belly.

"Spoken like a true military wife. I guess I was never lucky enough to find someone with a similar viewpoint. When I got orders, I had to find a new relationship."

"Guess you were hooking up with the wrong kind of woman."

When he held her gaze, the teen chatter faded. The firelight softened the angles of his face and emphasized the intensity burning in his gaze.

"I guess so." His deep voice beckoned. "But even an old Marine can bend every now and then."

She couldn't look away. Couldn't form words. A longing for something new with him tugged at her mind. Her family had started to settle. The tiny light at the back of her tunnel was not a train coming in the other direction. Which meant?

She could initiate a life independent of her family, a social life. Her stomach somersaulted. Only two ways to go on this: retch or fly. She pressed her fingertips against her mouth, but her lips tugged into a grin.

Aw heck, she was going to date Ryan.

CHAPTER TEN

NEVER CLEAN A LATRINE IN THE MIDDLE OF A SHITSTORM.

Ryan slapped his cap against his thigh. Too bad he didn't listen to his own advice. With a unit scheduled for deployment, he couldn't take leave. The competition terms didn't allow for crew replacements or reinforcements. Ava needed help on her farm and he needed to help her. So where was he going to find time to accomplish the work? The leather steering wheel creaked beneath his twisting grip. Something had to be cut.

Good thing Ava's project kept her busy every evening. A cold front and an inch of rain had turned the landscape around the Boundary site into a bog. Although he'd secured a Bobcat Skid Steer Loader to tear out the concrete and prep the land for a retention wall, he couldn't operate it in the mud.

His SUV fishtailed at the turn onto his street, Placid Court. He eased the accelerator. *Placid?* Now there was a joke.

The SUV slid to a stop. Beneath the glow of the streetlight, a powder blue Avalon sat parked in the middle of his driveway. Ryan pulled against the curb and shook his head. One person remained a constant in his crazy life, Mom. Although his expanded driveway could park three cars with ease, Mom always pulled in the middle of the slab the same way she tended to pull into the middle of his life.

He opened the unlocked front door. “Mom?”

Since he couldn’t enter his usual route through the garage and hang his keys on the peg by the door, Ryan pocketed the small keyring and moved toward the kitchen. Bent at the waist, only his mother’s bottom half showed from the refrigerator.

“Hungry?” He couldn’t resist stating the obvious.

She peeked around the door with her famous *mom look* that said his humor had missed the mark and although disappointed, she appreciated his effort.

“I haven’t seen you in a few weeks.” The rattle of bottles and plastic containers muffled her voice. “I figured if you were too busy to come over, I’d come to you.” She peeked around the side of the door. “I made cannelloni this afternoon. I already dropped off servings for Kim and Tracy. Do you want me to heat it up?”

“Thanks. I needed a meal for tomorrow—unless you haven’t eaten.”

The minute the words passed his lips, his error slammed into him.

She closed the refrigerator. The pleasant smile fixed on her face contrasted with the slight narrowing of her eyes.

Yep, she’d seen right through him. He had to hand it to her. Mom never gave up on a guy or her ideas for his future happiness.

“There’s a new elementary teacher filling in for Sheila Right while she has her second child. I heard she’s from Arizona so I bet she’s not going home for Thanksgiving.”

“Mom, I know you’re trying to help me out—”

"You're not getting younger."

"Thanks for the update." He clamped his jaw and switched on the single cup brewer. "If you made cannelloni for the family, you've been on your feet all day. Do you want a cup of tea? I bought a box of your favorite decaf."

"Sure."

He placed the pod into the device, and then opened the door to the screened porch. "It's mild this evening. Let's sit outside and listen to the rain."

Face it, Marine. She'd extract the truth, every morsel, every emotion, every probability. His mother Stella Murphy would put the Marine's finest interrogator to shame in less than two minutes.

"So," she started before he had time to sit down. "Have you seen Ava lately?"

He sank into his favorite deck chair. Since the cookout included the Robey family and Talley, it was an easy report. She listened intently, her gaze watchful.

"Sad case, raising four children without a husband." The soft glow of the porch light reflected in his mother's white hair. "The old Peter's place is more wild than farm."

Ryan relaxed against the chair back. At least she'd stopped with the dating list. But his mother was a Murphy and rarely gave up on an idea or an opportunity to promote her grandchild campaign.

"I know you carry the guilt for every man lost. That's one of the reasons I love you so much." She blinked rapidly at the sheen of tears misting her eyes. "You've got your father's heart."

He hugged her shoulders. "And yours, Mom." Which was the reason he hated to disappoint her, even when her constant matchmaking drove him crazy.

She caught a tear before it leaked down her cheek. "The

Robey family has been through a rough time. Children, especially boys, need a man's love and guidance. Tread gently and know your own mind and heart. They can't go through more hurt."

"Good point." He hadn't meant to add to Ava's problems. "I'll be careful. Thanks. I'm lucky to have a smart and generous Mom to keep my head straight."

"Wisdom comes from experience." She sipped her tea as if weighing her words. "When Ben died, we were all devastated. I lost a husband, a partner, and a friend. Kim and Tracy lost their dad. You lost the most." Her low, sincere tone tore at his heart. "You lost your way."

Although he'd never analyzed his loss, her analysis rang true for him and Robey's boys.

"It's hard losing someone you love, but a young boy?" She stared into her cup like it held the answers to the world's problems. "I'll stop by the farm again and offer my help to Ava and her family."

Where was his head? He'd been so consumed with his responsibilities and his attraction to Ava, the Robey boys' perspectives hadn't calculated. And that little girl? He fisted his hands. She wanted love and attention.

Standing in front of him, his mother waited. He scrambled to his feet and took her cup. Although she didn't speak, her tender gaze opened his chest and squeezed his heart. She blessed him with her love and wisdom every day. Today, she'd offered guidance. Looked like he needed soul-searching and an attitude adjustment.

WEDNESDAY EVENING, Ryan picked up a fast-food dinner and turned toward Ava's. The rain had lifted, but the lot needed another twenty-four hours to dry. Although the ceiling tiles had been delivered, the job site remained second on his stop list.

The crunch of his tires must've alerted the family because Ava met him on the porch.

"What brings you out this way?" She wiped her hands on a dish towel. "It can't be another tomato fight. Because of the rain, my boys have been riding the bus."

With her smile knotting his tongue, he shook the wobbly porch railing. "Are you ready for me to start on the porch?"

"I thought you had something going on after work too."

He did, but he couldn't stop loading his to-do list. Not in the shadow of her smile and the image of his sergeant. "I talked to my Marines about used furniture. Are you busy this weekend?"

Hair had worked free from her bandana. The silky tendril waved in the breeze urging him to touch it, let it slip through his fingers.

"We'll be home around this time for dinner," she was saying.

"My unit's collecting items for you."

"I...you...thank you." She shoved the tendril under the scarf and he sucked in his cheeks to prevent a groan.

"Maybe I can do something nice for the troops."

Walk in the room and smile might do it. Ryan straightened his spine and the goofy grin on his face.

"We'll shoot for Saturday, but I'll contact you later in the week to confirm. A lot of my Marines are single, so a home-baked pie or cookies would go a long way."

"You move fast." Her laugh died into silence. "I keep forgetting to keep an eye on you."

Actually, he liked the way she kept staring at him, especially when she thought he wasn't looking. But not when his head was bobbing up and down. Geez, she probably thought something was wrong with him. He straightened. No, sir. A woman didn't moisten her lips and stare at a guy's mouth if she thought something was wrong.

"I didn't mean to crowd you. The guys were complaining about too much stuff for their small quarters so I thought of you."

"No. I mean yes. I would love the items. The problem is storage."

"Is the barn dry?"

"One end." She led the way toward the lane, her slim hips luring him along like Toby following a bone. "When Mom and I moved in together, we had too much of everything. We repaired a section of the barn so we'd have storage for our excess."

She stopped at the barn entrance with her fingers pressed against her lips.

Although slim, her corded shoulders tightened beneath his hand. "Are you okay?"

She swiped at her wet cheeks. "Sorry. I haven't been in here since Mom passed. We replaced the roof on that side."

When she pointed, her hand shook. He'd done that. His big plan to help her had reminded her of losing her mother—as if she hadn't lost enough.

"We had a hard time positioning the first panel. I didn't think we'd get it. Then, boom, it clanked into place. I cried and Mom laughed. I mean a big belly laugh. I think I miss her laugh most of all."

"My dad's laugh was infectious too." He'd like to make Ava laugh like that. No doubt, she needed a reason to laugh. "Sometimes those memories sneak up on you. It sucks for a Marine."

Her eyes sparkled and then she let out a chuckle. Not a real laugh. But it was a start.

She jerked her chin toward the barn. "I'll show you the space I have left."

He'd been right about the farm crumbling around her feet. In the dark ages, red paint had lacquered the exterior. But years of hot Carolina sun had bleached the wood to a ghostly gray. An old roller door hung on one hinge, blocking the tractor entrance. Ryan grimaced. Great storage unit—for vermin.

Ava squeezed through a narrow opening below the lopsided door.

"How'd you get the furniture through here?" he said, half-talking, half-grunting.

The rickety hinges creaked and the wood shuddered from his shove, but he pushed through the crack she'd maneuvered without a stumble.

Ava pointed to the right. "We came in through the side door in the main part of the barn. I think it's sound, but the roof leaks. It was too high and steep for Mom and me to fix."

Inside the structure, the exterior light highlighted their shadows, emphasizing the size difference. Dust motes twinkled in the sunbeams like mini-flares. The smell of old hay and earth permeated the area.

Ryan pushed against the heavy timbers supporting the barn. "The foundation seems solid. Looks like you avoided termites."

"Even a blind squirrel finds a nut once in a while." She grinned. "My grandpa's favorite saying."

In his opinion she should hire someone with a frontend loader to put the old barn out of its misery. But it just didn't seem right to mow down her hopes, so he forced a half-ass grin. "What about rental space for the donations?"

Ava shook her head. "Not in the budget."

Of course not. "How's the loft?"

Based on the cobwebs stretched across old wooden beams

littered with nests, the critters liked it. A sharp object poked his rib. He blinked. In less than six-point-two seconds, Ava had gone from pleasant companion to warrior.

Her golden eyes glittered with fire. "Hold it right there. Are you suggesting—"

"You'll need materials for the roof." He kept his gaze high and tight. "If you don't use the loft, you'll need flooring. What did you use in the side area?"

"Pallets. We had to restore them, but they were free."

"Any left?" He moved toward the main part of the barn.

"You aren't listening."

Of course he was. He'd have to be deaf to miss the hiss of her breath. She was pissed, but so far he'd avoided an eruption. He crossed the aisle to the stall contents. A pile of steel roofing panels and an uneven pile of pallets filled the enclosure.

He whistled. "Gold mine."

Although her cheeks remained flushed, her glare had faded. "Materials are expensive and hard to find. Mom and I scored big with this haul. She said they'd come in handy. She was right."

"A lady with tools and the required building materials." He saluted her. "Ava Robey, you're one savvy lady."

"You're not too bad yourself. Good timing. You were two minutes away from being kicked off my land before that bit of praise."

Ryan sucked in his cheeks to suppress a grin. He'd been looking for the wrong kind of woman.

As if sensing his wayward track, she moved closer. "That doesn't mean I'm going to let you fix my barn roof."

He leaned closer. "Because?"

She narrowed her eyes. "Because it's too much. This is my barn."

"No argument there."

"I don't have the means to pay you."

"Understood."

She straightened and placed her hands on her hips. "Anyone ever tell you you're an infuriating man?"

"Not in those words."

"How would you feel if I came to your house and cooked and cleaned for a week?"

Okay, she'd surprised him with that one. "I'd be all over that—with one exception."

She stepped back. "You did that on purpose."

"I answered your question."

"That's not what I meant," she said. "Besides, I'm sure you mooch home-cooked meals from your mom."

"Not so much." He folded his arms over his chest. He wasn't going to discuss his Mom, unless— "Have you—" He cleared his throat. "Have you met my mother?"

"Yes." Ava glanced around the dank building like she expected an ambush. "When Mom was sick, your mother visited and dropped off a casserole."

Ryan stopped his head bobbing. Too bad, he couldn't pop himself on the back of the head every time the irritating habit occurred. "That would be Mom, always taking care of someone. But I'm past the age I want her to mother me. I love her." He swallowed to stop his dumb babble. "But... Could you come to Thanksgiving dinner with me? And bring the kids."

She froze. He stuffed his hands in his cammies. People usually liked a dinner invitation, especially with his mom's cooking. Then again, Ava might've heard about his mother's matchmaking.

"Ryan, that's family time."

"Hear me out. I know it's an unusual request." He raised his palms. "But this is a high value exchange for me. I'll fix the barn and your porch if you and the kids will come over for Thanksgiving."

She wasn't buying it. Trust seemed to be an issue with Ava Robey.

"Is there a problem between you and your mother?"

"Yes!" he said on a rush of air. "Every time I go over to the house, she tries to hook me up with another woman. Last month it was her new hair stylist. Now, it's a substitute teacher."

Laughter bubbled from her and he'd bet that's how her mother had sounded.

"I'm so sorry." She suppressed a giggle. "It's—

"Ridiculous! I feel guilty avoiding her." He raked his hand across his head. "Okay, how's the porch foundation?"

Ava followed him across the yard to the house. "There's five of us. That's too many people to pop in on a family gathering."

Ryan checked beneath the porch. She could use underpinning. He dusted remnants of dirt and grass from his palms. "No, it's perfect. Especially—" Aw man, he should have let it go.

"Especially?"

He huffed out a breath. "It gets worse every time one of her friends has a new grandbaby."

"You don't like babies?"

"Well, yeah. They're okay." Somebody should shoot him to put him out of his misery. "Mom wants more grandchildren, but I—" He grimaced. "I don't want to scare you. Maybe Robey never mentioned it. Stuff happens overseas. Sometimes Marines are exposed to carcinogens that could lead to birth defects. Dad was a doctor so that was a common dinner topic," he continued. "Who knows what exposure does to your genes, you know? With Dad's stories and my exposure in the Middle East, I decided not to risk fathering children."

Ava nodded, but she'd scrunched up her face. "It seems like an extreme reaction, but I won't fault you for thinking about the lives of others. I take it you haven't told your mother about this decision."

He shook his head. "Nah, I mean it's early. I haven't met anyone. But that's Mom's goal: more grandchildren."

He picked up a stick and threw it across the yard. Toby barreled after it. "Anyway, Mom loses her mind about my biological clock. So, if she sees me with you—"

"Yep, I'd say a date with five kids would do it. You're hoping she'll back off?"

He nodded. "That's why Thanksgiving dinner has such a high value for me."

"The mom-thing, I get. But there's always a risk of birth defects," she said. "Even with healthy parents."

"Maybe. But Mom—"

"I get it with moms. You love them, and you don't want to disappoint them. That's why it's so hard to tell them what you want."

He'd rather take another bullet than disappoint Mom... Ava had the kindest eyes. And he was an idiot. The porch railing wobbled beneath his weight.

"A free meal with this crew—" Ava grinned and he leaned forward. "As long as you're sure she's okay with three young boys who have endless pits for stomachs."

"Mom lives to feed the masses. I also gather guys from the base who don't have families or can't travel home."

She giggled.

"What?"

"It's hard to wrap my head around your tiny mother causing blind-date fear in a Marine who's fought terrorists."

Heat surged up his neck. As ridiculous as it sounded, facts were facts. "So, one meal at Mom's and we can call it square?"

"But—"

He raised his palms. "The barn and the porch. What else?"

"On your side, not mine." She pressed her fists to her hips. "I'm not taking unfair advantage of your family situation."

"Consider me a motivated buyer." He clamped his jaw and stopped his head from bobbing. "That's when you make the best sale."

"I only enter fair negotiations."

"It is fair to me. Stabilizing your porch isn't a big job and I'll get help for the barn roof. Trust me, a week of home-cooked dinners and providing a Thanksgiving buffer to defend against Mom's matchmaking is huge." Man, she had no idea how insistent his mother could be. "Amazing trade for me."

"I'm ripping you off." She crossed her arms over her chest. "Two weeks of dinners and the barn roof. My boys and I can handle the porch. But you'll have to come here for dinner. That way, it's only one more mouth and I can keep my kids on schedule."

"Works for me."

She thrust out a delicate hand. "Deal."

Her rough palm sent tingles up his arm. He rubbed his fingertip against his thumb and spun on his heel. He didn't know what it was about Ava Robey, but—

"Ryan?"

He squeezed his eyes closed and halted halfway to his vehicle.

"Talk to your mom. Don't let a day go by with something between you."

Ryan slid into his SUV and melted into the leather. Ava

had a spectacular way of blowing up his world. Hell, he'd helped her. Although she had a point about Mom, the barter — Where was his head? He didn't have time to fix her roof, her porch, or her life. He had a competition to win for Schmidt. In the meantime, he had a job at the base and a giant time management problem. Something had to give and it wasn't going to be a gritty little gal named Ava Robey.

CHAPTER ELEVEN

Thursday morning Ava hit the alarm so hard the tiny clock popped off the bedside table.

"No!"

She fumbled for the water bottle and eased the rasp in her voice with a long swallow. Although her schedule didn't allow for a Ryan date, her dreams did—until the stinking alarm interrupted them. With an unfeminine groan, she shuffled to the boys' room and opened the door.

"Rise and shine."

Moans, groans, and complaints filtered to the hall, but her tribe was true-blue. Despite his injury, Kyle had completed painting both bathrooms and tutored Whit. Nate and Whit had cleared the heavy debris from the storage room. Darling Hope had commemorated their progress in glitter paint crayons. Ava's sore muscles eased. Mercy, she loved them. This project had opened a window to their future. Her boys were growing into fine young men—way too fast.

After one hour and fifteen minutes of motivating the boys into motion, and whipping up a hot breakfast, she loaded the family into the Explorer for the drive to school. Wisps of low-lying clouds shattered the streetlight's glow with water droplets. Ava switched on the wipers, thankful her bid excluded exterior work.

"I should be able to knock out the cleaning today so we can start repairing drywall and trim for painting. Nate and Whit will be on drywall patching. Kyle, you can start painting the back room. I'll check again today in the daylight. But I think the walls are clean."

Nate pumped his fist. "Anything besides hauling crap to the dumpster."

"You are such a super weirdo." Kyle cuffed his brother's shoulder. "Consider it weightlifting."

Nate's brow knitted. "Says the guy who got to sit and paint."

"If you worked your arm as much as your mouth, we'd beat our deadline by two weeks."

"Guys." Ava wheeled into the middle school carpool line. "I know you're tired. So am I. Please, hang in a little longer. Once we finish the contract work, we can return to a routine."

Nate hopped out and slammed the door.

"What routine?" Kyle muttered.

Ava swallowed a response. She'd moved from Charlotte to provide the home-town atmosphere she'd experienced as a girl. Got that—until she'd put them to work. So much for new friends, and the guys who picked up the garbage didn't count.

At the job site, Ava cleaned to the whir of her thoughts. Their contract had given them a goal and a work ethic. Like hers, their social life had to go on hold. However, it was merely a delay not a banishment. They'd recover. The real issue was how to present her Thanksgiving plans to her children. Nate would focus on the food. Talley's presence would entice Whit. Hope lived for the limelight, more people to shower her with attention. But Kyle? She dumped filthy mop water down the tub drain. Kyle wouldn't be pleased.

The slam of a car door shook her from her thoughts. Mr. Butler wasn't scheduled to drop off the kitchen and bathroom tile until tomorrow. She rubbed her palms against her jeans and walked to the back entrance. The wide expanse of Ryan's cammie-covered shoulders accelerated her heart rate.

"How did you find me?"

Ryan raked a hand through his too-short hair. Her smile faded. He looked like a guy who expected a new watch for his birthday and received aftershave lotion.

"Accident. I was running an errand and saw your car. There couldn't be two Explorers with a dented rear fender in Sunberry."

Her breath caught in her throat, but his stern features didn't break into a grin at his joke. She moistened her lips. At least it had sounded like a joke to her.

"Are you in Butler's competition for the Main Street lease?" he said.

She ignored the strain in his tone. "Meet the head of Robey Contractors. I know we don't have the experience of the big guys. But we were delighted to make the cut. Main Street is perfect for Robey's Rewards." The man looked like he might be sick. "Are you alright?"

"Butler's competition?"

Since she'd answered his question, no sense in repeating a response. "I don't know what your deal is, but we do good work."

He started that nodding thing, but she wasn't in a generous mood. Men always thought they were the only ones who could lay a floor or replace a ceiling fan. She placed her hands on her hips. "Women can run contracting companies too. My sons are good workers. You've already seen that."

"I thought you were opening a shop in Jacksonville."

"Well, you *thought* wrong. I can't manage a business and make the commute back and forth with Hope in Kindergarten."

Okay, this was weird. He wasn't the only one jumping to the wrong conclusions. So if he wasn't questioning her ability, what had *stunned* him? You'd think he'd learned the sky was green instead of blue.

"Do you know anyone interested in this site?" She was chattering like a teenaged girl. But she couldn't seem to reel in her tongue. "When we finish the work, the place will be available for lease. It was a mess. I spent days removing junk. At first I hated the location, but it's starting to grow on me. I like the wood floors and with new paint..."

He did the nodding thing and she huffed out a breath. Although odd, the habit was all Ryan, which was more than she could say about his current behavior. It was like he'd suddenly gone alien. A sputtering sound leaked from her throat and she coughed to hide it. Ryan didn't move, stood beside his car rooted to the asphalt. When one of her kids turned that shade of green, they usually heaved on the floor.

"Ryan?"

"I'm your competition."

She blinked. The cleaning fumes must be getting to her. It almost sounded like he said— Random statements filled her mind. His project. His Marine buddy. She moistened her lips. "You want the Main Street property for Colonel Schmidt?"

"Right now, I'd like the ground to open and swallow me." He shook his head, his gaze distant. "I didn't know it was you until I saw that red Explorer."

Ava pressed her lips together. Yeah, she got the wish to drop through the Earth. It wasn't fair. They'd worked so hard. And since *when* had life been fair? But why Ryan—and Schmidt? The Colonel had already done enough damage to her family with his stupid car and his bully son. And she could just kiss a relationship with Ryan goodbye. Her boys would never forgive him for competing against them. They'd given up their weekends, their evenings, their lives to win the lease.

"I'll talk to Schmidt," Ryan said. "We'll find a different site."

"Not on Main Street. There hasn't been a vacancy since they renovated the Opera House." When she stepped closer, she noticed a tic twitched his cheek. Her fingers itched to touch it, touch him. She stuffed her hands in her pockets. Too bad they had to be competitors.

"I thought you were opening in Jacksonville." He rubbed a hand through his dark hair. "If I had known..."

She wasn't giving up. Her family had worked too hard. "I'm sorry for the Colonel. However, Robey's Rewards is important for my family too."

"This is messed up."

"I was hoping my competition was an elderly couple with hopes to turn an old dream into a retirement goal. But you?" A vile taste filled her mouth. "You're working to beat us, destroy our dream. Like you haven't done enough—"

"Ava, no." He shook his head. "I didn't know."

"But you still would've stepped into help a fellow Marine." A bitter laugh escaped before she stopped it with her palm. "That's what Marine's do, support one another."

"What are we going to do?"

Nothing. She wasn't quitting and neither could he. Too much was on the line—for both of them. So she'd continue like she always did when life kicked her too hard. She got up. And kicked back, *harder*.

"It's life. You didn't sign up to bail my boys out of trouble, but you did." She shoved a wild strand under her bandana. "I didn't plan to like you, but I do." *Just not so much at the moment.*

"I can't do this." He shook his head. "I've seen how hard

your boys work for you. I can't be the one to beat them out of that lease."

"It's a competition. You knew it going in and so did we."

Ryan narrowed his gaze. "Don't even— I'll find another way."

"You don't get to control the outcome. You don't validate our work." She took a deep steadying breath. "I'm competing. If that's a problem for you, talk to Schmidt. You made a commitment with him not me."

He was already shaking his head. "I can't compete against you and your boys."

"Can't or won't?"

"Why don't I beat the dog too," he muttered. "I can't take advantage of—"

"Of what?" She raised to her toes to get in his face. "A widow and her kids?"

"We made our decisions. Your boys didn't. We'll work something out."

"I've already worked out everything that interests me and so has your Colonel."

"Clear as day where your oldest boy gets his temperament," he muttered. "I wanted to honor Robey by helping his family."

Once, just once, she wanted to be tall enough to cuff a man. "Then do it. I'm holding you to your offer to fix my barn and deliver my goods."

The way he screwed up his features would've been comical if she wasn't ready to spit nails.

"I'm not in the habit of retreating."

She gave him her meanest glare. "Neither am I."

"And Thanksgiving?"

With the lease pressure ramping up, she didn't have time to socialize. "I gave my word. I'll honor it."

He moved forward. "Dinners?"

"Every night, my house, five-thirty."

When he turned to leave, her breath rushed from her lips like steam from a teapot. At his SUV door, he whipped around, his brows meeting in a frown. "Okay, for now," he said. "But I reserve the right to renegotiate if I come up with a better solution."

She chewed her lip to keep from grinning despite the anger boiling inside her. Good heavens, another man who had to get in the last word. She didn't want to consider what her obstinate son and his siblings would say about her interaction with Ryan.

Two hours later, Ava's cell signaled her to finish the work. In fifteen minutes, her sweet girl's day at Kindergarten ended. Her mouth dried. And her evening of explanations started. She dumped her bucket of filthy water into the sink.

Her boys would have a tough time swallowing her information. Ava locked the building and trudged toward her car. Which meant, she had to practice her sales pitch. Practice? First she needed to create one. Whit and Nate would be okay with attending the Murphy Thanksgiving celebration. Kyle, not so much. Her oldest would see right through it, and food wouldn't entice him.

Even after Ava had picked up Hope, driven home, and started dinner, a solid presentation hadn't formulated in her mind. She checked the chicken and vegetables simmering inside her slow cooker. Outside, the squeak of the school bus's brakes filtered through the silence. She held her breath, waiting for the thump of feet across the porch boards.

So should she bring up the issue before or after dinner?

Whit entered the kitchen. "Are we painting tonight?"

"We'll talk about our schedule for the rest of the week and the weekend." She poured milk into glasses.

"We're painting every night this week?" Nate entered.

"There's a game tomorrow night. I told some guys I'd be there."

Kyle dropped his bookbag on the floor with a thud. "Games are for regular kids."

Nate settled into his place along the bench. "Mom?"

Sure, son. Sounds like fun. Ava chewed her lip. "Let's see how far we get with the painting."

Hope climbed into her chair. "I washed my hands."

"Good girl." Ava placed a small glass of milk above Hope's plate. "I finished cleaning the windowsills, doors, and baseboards. I'll start cutting trim to replace the damaged pieces. Nate and Whit will start patching walls this evening. Kyle will paint a second coat on the bathroom."

Instead of presenting the news, she passed a plate of chicken and vegetables.

"So, we can go to the game Friday night?" Nate said.

Ava hesitated. With the competition they couldn't afford to take off. But she didn't have the heart to refuse. New school, new community. They needed time to integrate. That's the reason she'd moved her family to Sunberry.

"If we finish the patch work."

Nate pumped his fist. She cut Hope's chicken.

"If we go to the game, are you taking tomorrow evening off?" Whit said.

Ava blinked back tears. Leave it to her second son to ask about her. He had such a good heart, always thinking of others.

"I found out who we're competing against."

The scraping of silverware on glass halted.

"There you go, sweetheart." Ava moved Hope's plate near the table's edge.

Whit, intent as usual, waited. Nate held a forkful of chicken in the air. Kyle narrowed his gaze, suspicious of her explanation before she started.

She inhaled a steadying breath and gave them the news.

The minute she finished the explanation, Kyle's dark eyes narrowed. "I told you to watch out for Major Murphy."

"We can take him," Whit said. "I beat him clearing brush. And there's three of us."

Ava cleared her throat.

"Four," Whit corrected.

"Mr. Butler said the tile and grout will be delivered tomorrow." And her arrangement with Ryan? She opened her mouth.

"So, we finish the painting, and then start the floors," Whit said. "We can still beat the Major."

"Is there more chicken?" Nate asked.

"Geez, do you ever get full?" Kyle grumbled. "Most of the Boundary work is outside. With luck, the rain has put him behind."

"We can take him with or without a weather delay," Whit said.

"There's more." Ava stirred her food. "I bartered for a new barn roof with Ryan."

Whit didn't look surprised, but Kyle? The old anger pulled down his heavy brows. "What kind of barter?"

"Marines collected furniture to sell in our shop. The dry part of the barn's full."

"And in return." Suspicion laced Kyle's tone.

Even Nate had lost interest in his meal and was staring at her.

"Two weeks of home-cooked meals with us and Thanksgiving Dinner with his family." No sense in going for spin. She was running the household. But life was easier when her teens understood and accepted her decisions.

"We don't need his help," Kyle said.

"Yeah, we do," Whit disagreed.

"Thanksgiving dinner is at his mother's home. The

Murphy family, Michelle and Talley Frost, and Marines who can't get home for the holidays will be there," Ava said, taking advantage of the lull in the conversation.

"Awesome," Whit said.

Kyle set his glass down with a thud. "I have plans."

Nate scraped his plate clean with his fork. "I bet she's a good cook."

"All you care about is your belly," Kyle said.

"Enough," Ava said. "I accepted for all of us and we're going. I won't lose time cooking and we still get a fabulous meal." She caught each boy's gaze. "We'll go over for a nice dinner and then work at the site. With luck, I think we can finish the contract by the end of November. That means you can have an after-school life again."

Nate pumped his fist. "Yes."

Ava held up her palm. "Don't get too cocky. Once we open, I expect everyone to put in time on the weekends."

Although Kyle still scowled, he took his empty plate to the sink.

Within fifteen minutes they were motoring toward the job site. Behind her seat, Hope sang the Wheels on the Bus, but the boys remained quiet—no doubt, picking up on Kyle's sullen behavior.

"We're going to make this work," Ava said.

The uneven hum of Goldie's engine filled the silence.

Then again, maybe not.

CHAPTER TWELVE

He wasn't fit to sit on the floor with her dog, let alone join her family dinner. Ryan turned onto Ava's lane and bumped through the ruts to the front porch. Shadows highlighted movement inside the old farmhouse. Probably the boys. And he was the man who had judged them about their attitude. In fact, they'd been worried about Ava shouldering the work. Three teen-agers had vision and he'd been wearing night vision goggles on a day mission.

After killing the engine, he swung out of the pickup and slammed the door with a vengeance. How did he make this right? He'd made a commitment to a Marine in need. He couldn't back down from that promise. In the meantime he'd screwed Ava's plan. Yet, she held no animosity toward him. She'd accepted the news and moved on with the situation while he continued to crawl on the ground like a snake.

The hinges on the front door squeaked and Hope emerged accompanied by the big lab. Messy pigtails dusted her red coveralls and a timid smile deepened the dimple on her cheek.

"I colored a blue square at school today."

Kind of like the one boxing him in at the moment. He bent toward her. "I never was very good at staying in the lines."

She held up a paper with the blue box and Hope printed across the top. "Teacher says it takes practice."

He took the paper and nodded, matching her serious expression even though the kid always made him smile. "I'll keep that in mind. Is the smiley face from your teacher?"

Hope nodded. "It's for you."

Ryan folded the paper and placed it in his pocket. "I've got the perfect spot for your masterpiece."

Although she gave him a shy smile, she continued to twist her sneaker against the porch boards. "Do you ever give pony rides?"

Aha, he got where this was going. "When I was your size, I wanted a pony."

Her giggle sprinkled over him like liquid sunshine. "No, silly." She pointed at his back. "Up there."

"Ah, that kind of pony ride."

She nodded and he swung her up on his back. Small penance for his part in the competition. When he trotted around the yard with the big lab woofing behind him and Hope's high-pitched giggle spurring him faster, he half expected his feet to lift from the ground. But it was more than the child and the dog elevating his spirits. It was Kyle's surly attitude, Whit's compassion, and Nate's insatiable appetite. To top it off, Ava, determined and beautiful continually intrigued him. No wonder he couldn't stay away. Ava and her family created a total package.

"Giddy-up, faster."

Out of breath he raced toward the front of the house and halted, grabbing Hope's shifting weight at the last moment.

Ava stood near the porch rail. "Dinner's ready. Time to wash up."

He lowered Hope to the ground and climbed the steps leading to the kitchen.

"Mommy!" Hope raced up the rickety stairs. "Mr. Ryan is a bumpy horse."

"I see. Wash your hands and keep an eye on Nate. He was heading toward the kitchen table when I came out."

Hope nodded and sprinted inside, her dark curls bouncing.

Ava handed him a tall glass of lemonade. "Are you coming from the Boundary site or the base?"

He sipped the tart beverage, but it did nothing for the burning in the back of his throat. During deployments, bad situations surrounded a guy. Ryan's training prepared him for such events. His training wasn't doing squat for him now, not when he'd put Ava's business site in jeopardy.

Although his heart pounded in his chest, he kept his features neutral. "Base. I can't take leave until next week."

"I see." Her eyes picked up the reflection from the interior lighting.

He checked his boots. At least he wasn't tracking mud inside the house. "Have you told your boys about—"

"Yesterday afternoon."

That was to be expected. She impressed him as an honest woman.

"How'd they take it?" He opened the door for her.

"Pretty much as expected."

She must've sensed his stare because she turned and gave him a pointed look. Inside, the pretty glow on her cheeks accelerated his breathing. Crazy, what the woman could do to a man with a look. The refrigerator hummed. The old clock on the wall ticked.

"It would be easier to stomach if you and the boys were mad."

"Kyle's got that covered," she whispered.

When he entered the country kitchen with its long plank table, all eyes followed his movement. Seated along the long bench, Kyle, Nate, and Whit followed his entrance.

"They're really clean." Hope held up two pudgy hands for Ava's inspection.

"Take your seat." Ava opened the oven and removed a large glass pan. "Mr. Ryan's going to provide a status report."

Silence settled in the kitchen. Despite the amazing aroma of tomatoes and garlic, Ryan's mouth dried. Even Hope seemed to sense the importance of the question. Ava held out her hand for his plate.

"Did you go inside the Boundary property?" he asked.

A hint of amusement danced in Ava's hazel eyes. With her brick-colored Henley, they appeared honey-brown.

"But of course." She added a square of lasagna to his plate. "Since it was the only property that wasn't occupied, we had a good look."

"And the storage room?"

Her smile stayed in place. So, they both had looked at that twelve-by-twelve landmine.

"Was it bad?"

"Filled to the rafters with junk."

"Bad shake," Kyle said, although nothing about his tone indicated regret. "Since we got a late start, I wouldn't want you to gain an unfair advantage."

Whit lifted his milk glass. "Nothing like a competition among *friends* to spice up a job."

Nate grabbed two pieces of garlic toast. "So how far did you get?"

"One at a time," Ava said.

"We had a unit come in before the holiday, so... I'm starting this evening."

Kyle pumped his fist. "Too bad." Ava's grin faded and Kyle shrugged. "Hey, I'm for Team Robey."

"The winning team," Whit added.

"Actually, Mom," Kyle said. "It was a smart move having Major come over every night. That way we can keep an eye on his progress."

"Even—"

"A blind squirrel finds a nut once in a while," they added in unison.

The Robey laughter dissolved the stone cramping Ryan's stomach. Someday he'd make up for his unforgiving role in the family's drama. For tonight, he planned to enjoy the warmth of their home.

Ava's lips closed around a fork of lasagna. "What time do you plan to start work?"

The pink of her tongue traced her lips. He blinked. In Ava's presence eating was more than a means to survival. She chewed. He swallowed. Her lips tipped into a grin. He blinked.

"Work." Kyle's sharp word shattered the silence.

He had returned to the crosshairs of the Robey boys. Never reveal fear to the enemy. And right now. Right here. He was definitely outside the circle. What had Whit called it? Team Robey. Well, Team Murphy had strategy experience. In slow-planned motions, he picked up his napkin and wiped his mouth.

"I'm starting after dinner and plan to work until midnight."

"We enjoy a close match," Ava said.

"I respect Team Robey too much to slack off."

The boys' passed a knowing look down the line. The competition was on.

One hour later, Ryan bumped from Ava's lane to the asphalt and pressed Schmidt's cell number. Respecting the competition's terms didn't include finding alternate options. He had to find a come up with a strategy because he wasn't going to win Ava's lease from her.

"Major?" Schmidt's voice had an odd vibration in it. "Have you got good news for me?"

Ryan removed Hope's drawing and placed it on the passenger seat. No, he was depending on Schmidt giving *him* good news—like he was interested in another site or investing in a new parking garage and retail sites across from the Opera House.

"If it's dry tomorrow, I should be able to start removing the old drive and sidewalk."

Silence. The hairs along Ryan's arm lifted. "Schmidt?"

"That's a relief. Are we going to win the lease?"

We aren't competing. "If the weather holds, yes. But I've got a problem."

"Join the club."

Ryan shifted in his seat. Working with Schmidt was trickier than navigating a mine field. PTSD had messed Schmidt up, but he was still a Marine officer. By the time Ryan drove into the Boundary parking lot, he'd explained Ava's situation.

"I'm going to win." Ryan cut the engine. "I don't think we want to beat a Gold Star Family out of their chance to rebuild. We owe Robey that much."

"Tough break for Robey's family," Schmidt said. "But I'm not in a position to be generous."

Silence filled the SUV. Ryan turned up the volume. "Schmidt? Did I lose you?"

"Lana and I got into an...altercation last night."

Ryan gripped the phone. "What's that mean?"

"It means we need something to do, as in work. The boutique is a perfect solution. She can do the buying and chitchatting with customers. I'll handle the books and business side. "

Ryan thumped his forehead. "Did you make an appointment?"

"I don't need an appointment. I need a job for my wife other than hovering around me."

After fifteen minutes of denial, Schmidt signed off. Ryan slammed the car door with a satisfying pop. Marines always had to be tough guys. But they also dug in and kept fighting. Ryan had planted the seeds of change. With a few more weeks, he'd convince Schmidt or Ava that the Main Street lease wasn't the only deal in town. In the meantime, he needed to find the other deal.

CHAPTER THIRTEEN

THIS WAS RIDICULOUS. IT WAS A BUSINESS ARRANGEMENT, not a date. Ava checked the farm lane for Ryan's approach—for the fifth time in less than five minutes. A shiver of excitement trotted across her shoulders. No aches, no pains, no fussing. Her tribe would honor her commitment and host Ryan in an enjoyable and relaxing meal. She'd learn how he was progressing in the competition and spend down time with him. A piece of cheese slipped from her fingers. Toby gulped the morsel long before the ten-second rule applied.

"The Major is here," Whit announced.

Ava pushed her drying hair behind her ears and hustled toward the living room. Her stomach gurgled as the aroma of garlic, marinara sauce, and cheese filled the air. Toby's tail thumped hopefully—much like her pathetic heart. She turned to greet Ryan, hair wet and fresh from a shower. A new understanding of how the dog operated sunk in. And she absolutely would not beg for a piece of Ryan. Instead, she opened the screen and ignored the flashfire racing from her cheeks to her hair roots.

"Something smells good," Ryan said.

Ava squared her shoulders. He followed close, the heat from his big body warming hers, energizing her tired muscles to a steady hum. How many times had Josh followed her to the stove with those same words? Except tonight, guilt didn't accompany the thought. She straightened. It would be okay. Her recipe was delicious and while her boys harbored strong opinions, they had never embarrassed her—recently. Thirty minutes of harmony required two things: her boys' ability to accept Ryan and Ryan's ability to manage them. Yeah, and a star would rise in the east and camels would walk by.

"Table's set," Whit said.

Unlike Ryan's first visit, her sons didn't jockey for chair position. Kyle ignored Ryan, but he wasn't glaring at him. Hope watched him like Toby, hoping for a sign of affection. Whit and Nate seemed comfortable like he was a fixture at the table.

Ava huffed out a small breath and served a mound of vegetti topped with a plump chicken breast on each plate. With the final serving, she halved the tender chicken to share with Hope.

Ryan rotated his plate. "Ambrosia."

"I'm sure it's tasty. This is a family favorite." Ava dribbled dressing on her salad to keep from letting the compliment race to her head. "But ambrosia? That's pushing it."

Still, his compliment warmed her achy joints. She liked having an adult male at her table. The dressing bottle slipped from her fingers with a thump against the table. Ava held her breath, waiting for one of her offspring to comment. Only scrapes of cutlery on glass broke the silence.

In less than five-point-eight minutes, her sons polished their plates, pushed back from the table, and started cleanup—except tonight they omitted the belch contest.

"Nate, help Hope with her movie."

Five minutes later Ryan crisscrossed his utensils over his

empty plate. She stirred her zucchini but didn't lift her fork?

"It's nice this evening," Thank goodness her voice wasn't twittering like her heart. "Care to walk with me?"

She patted her lips with her napkin and stood. Not too bad—if she ignored the unusual husky quality to her voice. It wasn't like she wanted to get him alone so she could flirt with the man. She was merely checking out the competition in a polite manner.

When Ryan glanced at his watch, she rubbed her dry knuckles.

"Maybe for ten minutes." He winked. "Then, I have to go to work. Some lady and her tough crew are killing me."

What was with a simple wink? A guy closes one eye and something inside her melted down. It made no sense. Yeah, she wanted to beat him and win the lease. But for now, she wanted to walk around the pond.

Outside, a full moon illuminated the treelined lane behind the barn. He walked on her left, his heat and presence tingling around her. On impulse, she wrapped her hand around his arm.

"I love the tranquility surrounding this land."

He covered her hand with his and for once she didn't worry about her dry, rough skin or her cracked nails.

"North Carolina has some pretty country," he said. "I've traveled the world, but Sunberry brings me peace."

"My favorite childhood memories happened on this farm." She pointed to a weedy patch adjacent to the barn. "Grandpa always planted a garden over there. I tried to pick vegetables, but my harvest often included green tomatoes and the plant root. Grandpa had a low chuckle that seemed to come from his boots. He also had the patience of a saint."

Ryan released her hand and shook the rotted fencepost. "Agnus Rogers lives about a mile down the road. He has a tractor and might till your garden for a home-made pie."

The urge to spread her arms and spin on her toes flowed through her. This man, this place filled her with—joy. And pie didn't compare to the urge making her want to break out in song—not that she could carry a tune in a tote bag. Besides, her ability to formulate a suitable response crashed with the low timbre of Ryan's voice.

He was telling her a story about her neighbor. But his voice mingled with the whisper of the breeze crackling the naked branches and strummed her nerves like the strings on a guitar.

A shiver stepped down her spine. Chivalrous as always, Ryan wrapped a strong arm around her shoulders—which served to intensify the need coursing through her veins.

"With your fine cooking and fresh vegetables, you could open a restaurant." He skirted the garden and continued toward the pond.

When she touched his long fingers, he squeezed his arm to his body.

"Thanks." She stiffened at the responding hunger in her husky voice and cleared her throat. "But I have a family to raise."

"Good point. What if I hired you to feed me—long term?"

Laughter bubbled from her throat. While images of pulling him to the ground and running her hands over his chest filled her head, he was talking about food.

He shrugged, folding her hand in his. "I don't know how you made it or what was in it, but compared to my usual carry-out—"

"When my life slows down, I'll give you recipes and a cooking class." She didn't release his hand.

"My men and their wives might be interested in something like that."

The man never failed to surprise her. Even more surprising, she liked the idea. She liked most of his ideas. Around Ryan, opportunities kept surfacing. She wasn't sure how he did it, but she craved his optimism. Somewhere along her life road, she'd lost her enthusiasm. Maybe the passions she'd harbored in the past weren't dead. Maybe they were dormant—buried under loss and the trials of raising three boys and a baby girl. Maybe, the last terrifying depression tentacles had dissipated.

When he touched her hand, she leaned closer, matching her movements to his. For now, she wanted to savor the moment with Ryan. Besides, she didn't want to seem too eager about his suggestion.

"I'm serious." He bobbed his chin. "First, I'll confirm there's an interest. Marines can get testy if they display too much touchy-feely sh—er, stuff." The moonlight shadowed the strong planes of his face including a dimple in his right cheek. "But survival is a prime motivator. And if it's easy to prepare—" He snapped his fingers. "You've got a winner every time."

"Especially after a hard day working." Nothing like a set of toned shoulders to make a gal's heart go pitter-pat. *Focus, Ava. He's a competitor.*

"That's my strategy." She gave him her sweetest smile. "If I work the boys hard enough, they'll eat anything."

Ryan stiffened beside her. "I didn't mean—"

"I'm messing with you."

She shrugged, but her breath hitched like the time Grandpa laughed at her childish joke. But that didn't mean she'd forgotten her purpose. "Did you make progress at the Boundary site?"

"The place is cleaned out, but I still need to make a few runs to the dump."

"What about the suspension ceiling?" She held her breath.

"I should finish by Wednesday."

She swallowed. He was fast. But so was she. "What are your projections on the concrete work?"

The higher pitch of her voice almost drowned the croaks and peeps of the evening critters. Their wild song usually soothed her. It didn't tonight.

Ryan stepped in front of her and rested his hands on her shoulders. "I could slow down. I've got—"

Although she wanted to win the lease, wanted her boys to earn success, she couldn't let him waiver. Her strength had returned. Her family had pulled together, worked hard for their goal. And she was responsible for building that bond.

She wagged a finger at him. "We've had this discussion."

"You're killing me, you know that?"

She tipped her chin. "I'm meeting my goals."

"Would you let me take you to dinner instead?"

She halted. What? The smoky quality to his tone rekindled the heat she'd tried to control all evening.

"Too soon?"

Of course, it was! But not *his* response, *hers*. Everything about the moonlight, the memories, the land, him, hummed through her and pooled low in her belly. Ava cleared her throat. They were competitors. She'd demanded his full measure. Trusted him to fulfill that request. And she wanted more. Which was a recipe for disaster and heartache.

"You surprised me." Her voice wobbled. "That's all."

"Kyle doesn't seem as hostile."

They could discuss Kyle and the competition later. Now, was her time. Time to walk with Ryan, enjoy adult company, enjoy her femininity. Her hands curled into white-knuckled fists. But she couldn't. She'd demanded Ryan follow his duty. She had to follow hers—to her family.

She bowed her head and then pulled in a deep breath and met Ryan's gaze. "Not yet."

His brow furrowed, and a hint of disappointment shadowed his sideward glance. Or at least she hoped he shared her disappointment.

"Working together on the renovations has tightened our bonds. And Kyle's coming along," she added with a rush of words. "But we need more time."

She needed more time.

He stepped back, smoothing his hand across his pocket. "Will there be a time or should I stop asking?"

She bit her lip to keep from stepping into his embrace, to keep from asking him to hold her close, rub her arms with his big hands.

"Don't you dare give up on me," she whispered, her voice coming out more desperate than she planned.

He squinted at her, and his chin started the bobbing motion. "No, Ma'am. I'm not giving up. Just checking the lay of the land."

Just tell him. If he knew her secret fears, knew how far she'd come, he'd understand. She stiffened. That wasn't going to happen until she'd proven she possessed the strength to be the mother, the person, and the lover she longed to be. The decision was too important to make a mistake.

She moistened her lips. "Competitions and relationships could get messy." Still... "I'll take a raincheck."

"Don't forget about the furniture."

"Oh!" Ava pressed her fingers over her lips. The man kept her on her toes. She turns down a date and he comes up with more ways to help her. "I mean since you were busy with the competition—" She huffed out a breath. "I assumed—"

"With you, I never forget." His low voice edged with determination vibrated through her.

She extended her fingers to touch him and stopped. She couldn't test his tenacity. Her life depended on it—at least the life she dreamed of living.

CHAPTER FOURTEEN

Her crazy plan to heal her family was working. A weightless sensation threatened to float her to the ceiling fan. A common cause bonded them, refocused the sadness of the past to hope for the future. The competition with Ryan had strengthened their conviction.

It wasn't all lilacs and roses. Kyle had done the told-you-so speech about Ryan, but Nate and Whit had aligned with her and cut Ryan some slack. Now, everyone was ready to kick Ryan's tail and win the lease. Nothing like testosterone to turn a contest cut-throat. And she didn't care. They were happy. They were dedicated. They were engaged. So maybe—A tremor of excitement tickled her fingertips. She *could* accept a date with Ryan.

She slammed the trunk closed. "Hurry, guys. I've got to get home and get dinner on."

"Can I drive?" Kyle asked.

No, rose to her lips, but he'd worked hard. She held up the keys. "Okay."

"We're going to die," Whit muttered from the backseat.

"Mom!" Hope wailed.

"I was kidding," Whit said.

Ava turned to Hope. "Kyle will be very careful."

The ancient Explorer coughed.

"That didn't sound good," Nate said.

No! Ava balled her hand in a fist, but resisted shaking it at the sky. They'd had a *good* run going. It couldn't stop now.

"Press the accelerator to the floor once, count to ten, and turn the key." The last thing her son needed was to pick up on her shaky voice.

While Kyle followed her instructions, she held her breath. He glanced at her and turned the key. The engine coughed once and then hummed to life. She thumped the dash and the glove box fell open.

Kyle shot her a whatever look. "Once Robey's Rewards takes off, you need to buy a car."

"Goldie is perfect for a family with three teen-aged drivers coming up." She pointed forward. "Drive. And no Mario Andretti moves."

However, her son drove on the opposite spectrum of a race car driver. Tamping down the urge to tell Kyle to speed up, Ava gripped her seat while the quaint homes lining College Street crawled by her window. Five traffic lights separated the rental property from her farm. Every light turned red upon their approach.

By the time Kyle carefully signaled to turn into the farm, Ava's head threatened to blow off. The old shocks groaned with each rut in their land.

Kyle braked. "Are we expecting company?"

Her shoulders drooped and her grout-edged fingers beat with the rhythm of her brood's latest backseat argument. Goldie idled at her drive's entrance, exhaust clouding the back fender. Parked from the house to the barn, five trucks crowded the lane. Ryan's shiny black SUV headed the line.

Whit opened the door. "They're fixing the barn roof."

Hope scooted to the dirt and ran down the lane, followed by Whit and Nate.

Ava moved her lips, but didn't produce a sound. Ryan mentioned Saturday. But this? So many people and trucks.

Kyle opened her car door with an ear-deafening creak. "He's trying to get on your good side."

Absolutely, and he was doing a fine job of getting there. The ache in her lower back eased. Robey's Rewards had more merchandise. Her dream was unfolding from a budding idea to a family business.

By the time she'd walked to the barn and joined Hope, Nate, and Whit, her brain lost the morning-after binge fog. Tall, wide-shouldered, with a big smile stretching his features, Ryan approached her.

She'd refused a dinner date with that beautiful specimen of a man. And sometimes she made uninformed decisions. Ryan's toned torso and lean hips, accented by a long-sleeved black t-shirt and jeans, beckoned her. Ava blotted her lips with the back of her hand. Phew. Mothers did not drool in front of their children.

Ryan didn't just look good. He'd rounded up a team of men, collected merchandise, and fixed the barn—for her. Not because he thought she couldn't. Because he wanted to do something for her. When a shiver of excitement traveled down her spine and magically dissolved the ache above her right hip, she clenched her fists.

"Hey," he said.

"Wow!" she managed with a sudden rush of air.

He did the nodding thing she was growing to like. "Wow?"

"I didn't expect...I mean, I knew. It's just...This is way more than I imagined. Thank you."

He ran calloused fingers up her arm. "What's the status on College Street? Are you going to make me sweat?"

I hope so. "First coat of paint in the kitchen and the front area completed," she said, delighted with the distraction and the chance to spotlight their accomplishments. "You?"

"Some hard-hearted lady held me to an offer to fix her barn, so I'm running behind. But I'll catch up."

"Better hustle." That couldn't be her voice. She'd never smoked.

"I ordered pizza to feed the men. Want to join us?"

She mimicked his nod because for a moment she doubted she could speak. "Absolutely. Do you need drinks, silverware?"

"I brought a cooler. But if you have an old tablecloth, that would be helpful."

In the house Ava washed her face in the kitchen sink because Kyle had commandeered the bathroom. No doubt, she still had paint spatters masquerading as freckles. However, Ryan had already witnessed today's damage, up close and personal. A tingle raced along her fingertips at the memory of his touch, his look, him.

Outside the kitchen window, Ryan's ten-men crew crafted two makeshift tables with sheets of plywood. Her heart spun in her chest. She was going to a party. Not a kid's birthday party, which didn't count, but a party. Too bad the men hadn't brought their wives. Maybe in the future.... *Party today. Back to work tomorrow.*

Still, she was attending a celebration. Feeling like a schoolgirl at her first dance, Ava rifled through the linen closet and selected two flat sheets to serve as a tablecloth. From the counter she gathered the last roll of paper towels and a sleeve of Paw Patrol cups from Hope's last birthday.

Ryan met her halfway to the picnic tables and pulled his sensuous lips into an exaggerated frown. "You washed off the paint spatter. I liked it."

She laughed to hide her body's inappropriate response. *Dang, the man.* He was like the stupid TV bunny that kept going and going.

"Tomorrow, I'll add purple or maybe orange."

"Works for me. Come on." He held out his hand for hers. "I want to show you something before we eat."

His long fingers encircled her hand—callouses rubbing callouses. Her breath hitched.

"We used every steel sheet you had to fix the roof."

The last of the daylight filtered through the shrinking wood of the barn walls. Voices and laughter faded. The faint odor of animals and earth tickled her senses. But the primary scent of man permeated the air. He led her to the back of the main area.

She blinked. "All this stuff."

"Yeah."

He turned to her and ran his fingertips along the sides of her arms. Shadows emphasized his intense gaze and air went into short supply. She struggled to draw a breath. He leaned closer, his spicy scent filling her senses. His breath with a hint of yeast, mingled with hers.

"I've been thinking," he said. "Two weeks of your cooking doesn't seem to be adequate payment."

"You want three weeks?"

The light glinted off his teeth. "I wouldn't turn down another week. However, I was thinking on the lines of a kiss. Would that be okay?"

Because her mouth refused to obey her commands, she nodded.

When his lips, warm and firm, pressed against hers, her lids drifted closed. His toned shoulders teased her fingertips. Worries about responsibility, competition, depression, and kids vanished. She pressed him closer. His body heat scorched cheek. The thump of his heart vibrated against her chest. Raspy breaths filled the silence.

He ended the kiss long before she was ready.

"Well, maybe this," he murmured.

While his hands drifted down her hip to her backside, the soft brush of his lips intensified. With splayed fingers he snugged her against him so she molded to every nook and cranny of his body. Her heart fluttered. When she gulped air, his tongue swept inside her mouth. Soft and warm, it shot electrical jolts to her fingers, toes, and unspeakable places. A moan leaked from her throat and he seemed to interpret her guttural sound as approval.

He wasn't close enough. Too many layers of clothes separated them. Fabric hid the coarse hairs on his arms, the turgor of his veins, the cords of his muscles. Too soon, he ended the kiss, but didn't release her. With the sound of ragged breathing filling the silence, he held her close. A frantic heartbeat pounded in her chest, but she wasn't sure if it belonged to him or her, maybe both.

"I figured it would go something like that."

His breathless voice surrounded her and she scrambled to speak.

"That doesn't get you off the hook for another week of home cooking." His heart-stopping grin turned her argument into mush. "But don't go all wildcat on me if I steal another kiss."

Wildcat? Oh, he didn't know the feral being inside her clawing to get out. Besides if she unleashed her urges, he'd be closer, not further away. From the backyard, Hope's youthful giggle filled the silence. Ava froze and he released her.

"In case you've forgotten, I have four children."

"Hard to miss them." He winked. "But harder to miss you."

One minute longer, just one—to flirt, touch, continue what he started and she craved. And what would she say if one of the children finding her wrapped around Ryan like a vine on a fencepost? Heat warmed her cheeks.

"Kyle and I had a heart-to-heart." Her words rushed from

her lips, but she needed to talk to suppress the desire no mother of four should consider.

Even with her son's declaration fresh on her lips, her hands drifted to the front of his chest. A jolt of need shimmered down her fingertips and triggered a low burning in the pit of her belly. For a moment she hesitated, enjoying his embrace. Another laugh from outside filtered into the silence, closer this time. She forced leaden feet to move back two steps, a memory of Kyle's worried expression filling her mind. Family and business. She'd already done her five minutes of hussy.

"He's trying to fill Josh's shoes." Her throat seemed to close on her words. "Trying to be the man of the family."

Ryan nodded, but it was slower, more intentional. "Poor kid. Nothing worse than the time between a boy and a man."

"I've got my son back. He's talking to me again. Telling me what keeps him up at night. I was so afraid I'd lost him."

Ryan touched a tear in the corner of her eye. "Frustration can do strange things to a man."

And a woman. She swallowed. The gentleness of his touch, the tenderness in his voice tugged at her. When she smoothed her trembling hands down the front of his t-shirt, his abs rippled beneath her palms.

"He's coming around." Ryan took her hands in his and kissed her knuckles. "Cut yourself some slack."

Oh, she wanted to cut more than slack. She wanted to cut loose, forget about children, bills, and responsibilities, enjoy her womanhood and Ryan. Immerse in him without a care in the world. A huff of regret slipped past her lips. But she wasn't free. She couldn't risk her relationship with her children. Her shoulders drooped. She'd lost one man. Had almost lost herself. And she was no longer that broken woman. Maybe she was strong enough to balance her children and Ryan.

She placed her palm against his cheek, loving the rasp of new growth on his strong jaw. “Mothers rarely get the luxury of slack. But so you know,” She ran her thumb against his mouth. “Your kiss made me feel very greedy.”

His lip lifted, sending a flutter in the most indecent place. He canted his head as if asking permission.

When she nodded, he brushed her lips with his. “You’re like sugared pecans. Can’t eat just one.”

“So you’re comparing me to nuts. Hmmm, not sure if that’s complimentary.” She tried for humor, but sounded like she’d eaten rocks.

“There’s something between us.” He nibbled at the side of her mouth, driving her crazy. ”It was there from the first time. But that was before I kissed you—”

“It was a nice kiss.” She stepped back before she jumped up and wrapped her legs around his waist.

“Nice?” But he didn’t sound offended. “I had a different description in mind.”

“All right. Does hot work for you?”

His breath whistled in the stillness.

“Yes, ma’am. I’d say that pretty much defines what’s happening on my end. I’ve got a weekend of hard work. Then, I’d like to make good on that dinner invitation you had me put on hold.”

“I was hoping for another kiss.” She dropped her gaze to his mouth. So much for stepping back. He had a sexy mouth. Full, firm lips. Strong jaw. Nice teeth. Then, there were the dimples.

While his lips brushed hers, his rough palms cupped her chin. Amazing such a big man could have the gentle touch of a child.

“I anticipate finishing next week,” she whispered.

He kissed her again, light, but lingering.

“I’ve come up with a way everyone can win.”

"No!" Why'd he have to spoil the moment? "You're worse than my boys," she added to soften her refusal. "Never give up."

"If I had given up on you, I couldn't do this." He kissed her again. This time he pressed his tongue against the seam of her lips. She accepted him, her breath quickening with her heartbeat. His playful, insistence of quick parries heightened her awareness, increased her urgency to match him stroke for stroke. She nipped his tongue. He pulled back and she winked.

"That would've been a sin. You and your Marines have already helped us with new inventory and storage. But the rest must come from my children and me."

He nodded. Her Marine understand moderation, ways to make the goal fun. No doubt, his methods made him a good officer and a good man. When he stepped back, resignation, not anger fired his gaze.

"Yes, ma'am," he said. "Some things a person needs to accomplish on their own. But I'm not a man to give up."

Although unsure what he meant, she didn't want to argue. "Thank you."

The low whispery quality of her tone surprised her, but her words were sincere. Ryan Murphy was an unusual man. At least unusual in what she'd observed in her thirty-five years.

When she grasped his hand and turned to leave, his long fingers caressed hers. He didn't move, forcing her to turn back to him. Behind him, a single beam of light penetrated a knot hole. Dust motes glittered around him. She forced her gaze to meet his. Based on the gleam of his amazing eyes, the spark igniting her had touched him too.

"My pleasure." His tone said he'd make sure they both enjoyed it. "For now, we're running neck and neck. About that dinner? We could consider it a cease fire—for a night."

She stepped back. “You’re a temptation, Ryan Murphy. I’ll give you that.”

“And dinner?”

“After I beat you in the competition.”

He caught her in one stride. “Our dinner date will be a celebration of my win.”

She bolted through the tiny opening. “In your dreams, Marine.”

CHAPTER FIFTEEN

HOLIDAY TIME.

Ryan whistled a tune on the drive to Ava's farm. Mother Nature had created the perfect Thanksgiving afternoon. Blue sky backdropped the last brown leaves of fall and a mild fifty-eight degrees bathed the North Carolina coast. And he was *way* too cheerful about the holiday. Sure, he liked family get-togethers, especially with Ava running interference from his meddling relatives. But that didn't explain his near-euphoria. It wasn't like he'd hit the stupid lottery. Not good. Not good at all.

He tightened his grip on the steering wheel and veered right to bypass a pothole. Until he found investors, humor was a luxury. Without them, Ava wouldn't have a place for Robey's Rewards. Without funding, he'd have to live with beating her out of her dream. He hit the signal lever so hard it bounced against his palm. His SUV bumped up the lane to Ava's home.

Despite the saggy roofline and the peeling paint, Ava's old farmhouse eased the pinch in his shoulders. A soft breeze moved the swing where he'd first sat with her. She'd been so strong and determined. He squared his shoulders.

She'd have her dream of opening Robey's Rewards—*if* she'd agree to his proposal. The location across from the Opera House met her criteria. Leasing space below a new parking garage shouldn't send up red flags. However, postponing her opening for a year might kill the deal. He'd bring it up—soon. But not today. Today, she'd enjoy a nice dinner with his family and with him—his thanks for helping him mend the rift with his mother.

The front door swung open and Hope, dressed in a brown dress with a turkey on the front, charged down the steps with the big lab bounding behind her.

He swung her into the air. "Hey!"

Her brown eyes sparkled with excitement. "We're going to a party."

"I know."

"And we're going to have turkey. A real one that doesn't come in a bag."

The kid could always make him laugh. "Which brother told you that?"

"Nate. Kyle says he's always hungry."

Ryan set her on the ground and she trotted beside him, chatting about her latest discussion with one of her brothers.

Whit pushed open the front door carrying a foil-wrapped dish. "Mom's still getting ready. I'm supposed to put her persimmon pudding in the floorboard, navigator's seat."

Hope tugged him toward the front door. "It's really good. Grandma used to make it. She can't make it anymore because she died."

"Geez, Hope." Whit shook his head and slammed the SUV's door.

A furrow formed in Hope's brow. "She did. Now, Mom made it for us. We'll share it with you."

Inside, Ava waved from the hall. "Happy Thanksgiving. Kyle, did you change your dressing?"

Nate joined them from the kitchen, a stack of graham crackers in his hand. "I bet your mom's a good cook."

The front screen slammed behind Whit. "Sorry, Major. Mom teaches manners. They don't listen."

"It was a compliment," Nate protested.

Whit pointed at Nate's leg. "Change your jeans. Mom said no holes."

"This is the only pair that fits."

"Wear your khakis."

"No way. We're not going to church."

"Boys!" Ava entered the room. "Can we go through one day without argument, please?"

Ryan straightened. One of these days she'd enter a room and he'd breathe like a normal Marine. Today, wasn't the day. Dressed in black slacks and a maroon sweater, Ava hurried into the midst of her unit. His fingers tingled with a need to touch her.

"Almost ready." She bent to adjust the frilly edge of Hope's dress.

You'd think he'd remember to keep his eyes front and center around her, but nope. His gaze followed her downward. He clamped his jaw tight to prevent a noisy exhale. Nothing wrong with the curve of her backside. Those snug pants didn't leave a lot to his imagination, which was running about as fast as Hope's mouth.

Of course, Kyle shot him a 'back-off" gaze, but the teen's expression lacked hostility. Ryan kept his features stoic even though his right arm flexed with an internal fist pump. The kid was coming around. Even more crazy, Ryan had predicted the teen's behavior. Too bad, he hadn't predicted his.

His self-talk about meeting his duty to a fallen Marine had worn thin. Sure, he was attracted to Ava. She was a beautiful woman. But his mercurial behavior, his willingness to risk everything he'd worked for— He snapped his slackened jaw closed before she noticed his dumb expression. Her brows formed a little v above her hazel eyes. Aw, man she'd crawled under his defenses and captured his heart.

"Are we ready?" Ryan said. Because he needed to move to keep from thinking.

Ava retrieved a small black leather bag from the coat closet. "Whit, did you—"

"Dessert's loaded in the floorboard, navigator's seat."

"Thank you."

Hope grabbed his hand and hopped beside him to the car. "I want to sit behind Mr. Ryan."

Ryan folded down the second row of seating. "Here's the special girl spot." He helped her inside. "And you can sit on my side of the car. How's that?"

Hope blinded him with a radiant smile. "It's my size."

By the time he'd tucked Hope into her seat, Ava had already opened the passenger door. She glanced over her shoulder and his heart stuttered. "Sorry. It's like this when we go somewhere."

"Keeps life interesting," he said.

"I'll remind you of your description on the way home.

"I hope everyone's hungry. Two Marines I expected to join us made last-minute plans, so we'll have to pick up the slack."

"Nate has that covered," Whit muttered.

"And me." Hope waved her arm in the air.

"Oh, heavens," Ava said. "I hope your mother understands the impact of her invitation."

"She'll love it." And so did he.

BY THE TIME he turned into his mom's driveway, the shock of Ava without coveralls and his lunatic thoughts had worn off.

"How many people are coming?" Ava asked.

Seven cars crowded the curved drive to the white two-story brick home.

"We expect two dozen, maybe more."

"Talley's here." Whit opened the back door. "That's their SUV."

Nate made a kissing sound. Kyle laughed. Ryan caught Whit's glance in the rearview and nodded. It wasn't much, but a man needed to know he wasn't alone. Heavy drama accompanied falling for a woman.

When he stepped outside, the crisp fall day and the proximity of his family home slowed the buzz inside him. Returning to the place and the people who shared his history, filled his well—and the last week had nearly drained it.

Hope trotted to the magnolia dominating the front yard.

"That used to be my hideout," he called to her. "I waited in the branches to surprise my dad."

"Like this?" She disappeared amid the remnants of brown leaves and giggled.

"This must have been a wonderful place to grow up," Ava said.

"It's not just the house and grounds. The people of Sunberry also make it home." He took the dish from her hands. "Your boys will settle in. You've made a good decision to come back."

Ava's smile wobbled. Soon, he'd smooth the worry from her brow—if his plans unfolded.

"It's a beautiful place. " Ava stepped around the pots of bright yellow and orange flowers on the steps.

"And lots of work. I used to mow the lawn every Saturday." He opened the front door. "Happy Thanksgiving. Incoming!"

Inside, the hum of voices, clatter of glass and utensils, and aroma of roasted turkey and ham washed over him in waves. This house, these smells, these people, said home.

Within seconds his mother moved into the foyer. Although Stella Murphy stood no more than five feet tall, she seemed to be everywhere, like a tiny sandstorm whirling from all sides.

She wiped her hands on an apron sprinkled with orange and yellow leaves. "Happy Thanksgiving."

Uptight, his teenage guests looked like new recruits on the first day of boot camp. But leave it to Mom to ease their concerns. She hugged each Robey member to her ample bosom creating a crooked smile even on Kyle's unlikely features. Within minutes, she'd found playmates in the shaded backyard for Hope, and a football game for the boys.

Then Mom turned to Ava. "As soon as Ryan shows you around, I'll give you a job." Stella gave him a knowing look. "All who enter become part of the Murphy clan. It takes a lot of working hands to feed this group."

He'd thank Mom later for a few minutes of alone time with Ava. Her calloused fingers intertwined with his and he almost kissed her knuckles. Instead, he led her to the back door. "I'll give you the nickel tour."

In the yard by the fence, Hope and CJ, one of Ryan's many cousins, climbed the ladder on an oak with a trunk wider than three men.

"Is that the famous treehouse you built with your father?" Ava asked.

"Yes, ma'am." He shaded the sun with his hand, but his eyes still watered. "Dad said we had to build it right so the next generation could use it. Looks like we accomplished his goal."

Hope and CJ waved from the structure nestled high in the thick limbs.

"Be careful," Ava said.

The kids would be fine. But with the sunlight highlighting Ava's hair, the spark of laughter in her eye, and the curve of her smile, delusions attacked him. An image of a family with Ava blossomed in his mind.

"It's like Swiss Family Robinson." She tipped her head back, exposing the smooth flesh of her neck.

Say something, Marine. Tell her how pretty she looked with sunlight dappling her hair, or how the chip in her tooth winked at him, dared him to touch it with his tongue. He moistened his lips and gently squeezed her fingers.

"I bet the first time you took your nieces and nephews up was a lot of fun."

He stumbled. Not the same as following his own son up the ladder. That dream had died long ago. Ryan shook his head. It was crazy he still harbored that old dream. Maybe that's why he enjoyed working with Nate and Whit.

A furrow grooved the space between Ava's eyes.

"I, um, talked to Mom like you suggested." He hadn't planned to tell her. It seemed like a dumb subject for a grown man. But right now, he'd go for dumb over crazy. "You know about pushing women at me."

"Ah."

"I was afraid to tell her." Heck, the old fear of approval still rattled his bones. "I didn't want to disappoint her. She's always been there for me. Sometimes, too much," he added. "But I'd rather take a beating as disappoint her."

"How'd she take it?" Ava said.

"We cleared the air. She knew I was avoiding her."

Ava made a face and he bit his lip to keep from grinning. She'd make a terrible poker player, but her different expressions cracked him up. Life around her would never be dull.

"Good thing you said something. You never want to let the sun set on a disagreement, especially with your mother."

He followed her gaze to their joined hands and stopped

rubbing his thumb back and forth over her knuckles. *Don't let go.* Robey's last words settled in his mind. He'd been rubbing her hand the same way he'd rubbed the stone. In Afghanistan the stone had saved his life, given him something to hold onto, focus. Touching Ava had the same effect—except better, far better.

"After Mom passed I rehashed every disagreement we had." She did a cute little shrug, but didn't mention he was an idiot. "Most of them weren't that important."

"People get wrapped up in the details." He still did—still was. "Sometimes we lose sight of the important things, like me and Mom."

Like what happened with Ava. When she was near, battle-field images faded. She looked ... perfect, half teasing, half-flirting one moment and kind the next moment. The different sides of her kept him guessing what was next. Her lightheartedness seeped into his soul. Urged him to climb into the treehouse with her laughing behind him.

"I try to remember that when my sons get out of line." She moved toward the house.

He followed, hoping she'd remember her words if he got out of line, if his plan didn't work out. His smile faded.

"Deployment has a way of changing your perspective."

Ava stopped and turned back to him. "I'm sure it does."

He held out his arm and she threaded her hand around his forearm and squeezed. He covered her small hand with his.

"It's a beautiful day. Our families are healthy and happy." Her warm smile shocked his heart into sprint mode.

"Thanksgiving," he murmured.

Although Mr. Simms, the town octogenarian, could've outwalked him around the family home, within a few minutes their time alone ended. Ava joined his mother in the kitchen and he was ordered to home-made ice cream duty.

When he glanced back at Ava, his mother motioned him

to leave. Mom's house. Mom's rules. Besides, Ava could handle his mother's gentle probes.

On the patio Ryan sat on the stool and cranked the old churn. He'd purchased an electric replacement five years ago and Mom had donated it to the base. When he questioned her choice, she'd smiled and said, *Murphy tradition.* At the time her response didn't make sense. Families mattered, and family traditions connected the generations. What would it be like to develop traditions with Ava and her family?

A long bank of windows faced the patio providing the perfect position for kitchen surveillance. Ava, with a perpetual grin on her face, filled glasses with ice, and chatted with his sister Tracy. Although they'd never met before today, they laughed like old friends.

Peace settled around him. He'd brought Ava home, the same way they'd all come home. The Murphy gathering would resemble a Robey meal with multiple conversations, shared events, memories, and dreams.

Despite the chilling interior, the handle turned easier. A family to guide and watch grow wasn't out of reach for him. Ava caught his gaze, smiled, and lifted her hand before turning back to her task.

No, Marine. It was right in front of him.

CHAPTER SIXTEEN

Inside the expansive Murphy kitchen, Ava's heart fluttered faster than the mixer whipping the potatoes. She'd accepted Ryan's invitation because he'd been desperate for a companion and she'd been desperate for a nice family holiday. Her plan did *not* include an education on the makings of a gentle hero who'd grown up in a loving family. Ryan understood the value of relationships and family tradition, components she'd struggled to provide for her children.

He'd be a fantastic role model for her sons. The strong warrior blended with the gentle mentor—a man she could see herself loving. She stiffened. *Slow down.*

Hadn't she learned anything in the five years since Josh died? Strong women and their families survived. Weak women couldn't support and provide for their children. She'd fought too hard to regress. Not even for a day? Not even when Ryan had given so much to her and her family? Not even when he was troubled and needed support too?

"The feast is prepared," Stella announced in her soft but commanding tone.

Within moments the TV silenced and family members drifted toward the dining room.

Outside Ryan stood, his blue plaid shirt rolled to the elbows, exposing powerful forearms. When he extracted the stainless center of the churn, corded muscles flexed. Ava's belly squeezed, and it had nothing to do with the aromas drifting through the house.

Michelle Frost turned an immense mixing bowl on its side and Ava ladled hot creamy potatoes into the serving dish. "I love the Murphy celebrations and so does Talley."

Ava swallowed. Mom and Josh would've loved this dinner —just like the missing member of Michelle's family. "Is your husband deployed?"

Michelle's smile faded. "It's always one of us."

"If you ever need another woman to talk to, give me a call —anytime."

"Thank you. I'd like that." Michelle placed the dirty bowl near the sink. "I've thought about calling since our infamous hospital meeting."

"That's a day that'll go down in Robey history."

"Ryan felt so bad about the accident."

Ava added a serving spoon to the potatoes. "Kyle didn't have permission to use the chainsaw. If he had followed instructions, it wouldn't have happened."

"It doesn't matter." Michelle's eyes sparkled with unshed tears. "Saying you did your best doesn't cut it. In the end, the officer is responsible."

"You and your husband are officers?" Ava selected her words. "It must be hard to be responsible for the lives of others."

"You never get over the loss of other Marines." Michelle lifted the serving bowl. "I think they're waiting on us and the potatoes."

At the dining room entrance, Ava halted. In the time it

had taken to whip the potatoes, Stella had orchestrated a transformation. The long table, adorned with a festive tablecloth and matching placemats and linen napkins, stretched farther than the plastic structures used in her childhood cafeteria. And the mountains of food? Even her youngest male couldn't eat his way through such a feast.

"This is not a family dinner," Ava murmured. "It's a community banquet."

Stella's laugh filled the room. "Ryan's father loved people. He was always inviting someone to dinner."

"They had to knock out a wall to get the table into the house." Ryan pointed halfway down the length of the food-laden table. "From that sixth chair to the end used to be the living room."

Ryan held her chair.

She held up her index finger. "Hope."

Stella pointed toward a small table with four chairs, crammed in the corner of the room. Hope and her red-headed friend sat with Talley and Whit.

"Sit, enjoy," Stella said, her face flushed from the warmth of the kitchen but also the warmth of her heart.

When everyone had settled at the table, Stella directed them to link hands. Michelle, seated near the end of the table, took Whit's hand to connect the small table and complete the circle.

Ava sucked in a shaky breath and Ryan rubbed her fingers with his thumb. Although she'd missed Josh's presence, Ryan, not Josh, comforted her. Would she always doubt Ryan—wonder if he'd been better, more alert, she wouldn't be a widow? Kyle wouldn't be angry. Whit wouldn't be hypervigilant. Hope wouldn't cling to every nice male role model. Nate wouldn't try to eat his way through the loss. And what about her? Once she put the past to bed, didn't she deserve a life, happiness, fulfillment with a man? With Ryan?

At her side Ryan's calf grazed hers. Like her, Ryan was a package deal. If she agreed to date him, this big wonderful family might become a part of her family's life. But could it make up for what Ryan had taken away from her, from her family?

At the head of the table, Stella's voice quickened. "Cancer taught me to treasure every day I'm alive, and I'm grateful to all of you for sharing this day of thanks with me."

Ava stiffened. Ryan had never mentioned his mother was a breast cancer survivor. With the ending of the prayer, the clatter of utensils and multiple conversations filled the room.

While Ava spooned food on her plate, missing pieces of the Murphy puzzle spun in her mind. Ryan had been in Afghanistan five years ago with Josh. She chewed the moist turkey, so tender it should melt in her mouth. She sipped her water. A missing piece haunted her, and she intended to find it.

On the ride home Ava leaned against the headrest. Behind her, the boys talked about the dinner in low tones and Hope, exhausted from playing with new friends, slept in the third seat. Ryan glanced her way, but his dark sunglasses obscured his expressive gaze.

"Thank you for sharing your family with us."

"They're good people." He grinned showing a dimple in his right cheek. "A little weird at times and meddling. But they always stand behind me."

"A trait you share. I didn't know your mom had breast cancer."

"Yeah, that was a scary time for all of us," Ryan said. "Sometimes it still is."

"It never goes away." At least it hadn't during her mother's illness. "How long has it been?"

He glanced away from the road, his dark brows pulled together. “What?”

The blinker clicked indicating the farm lane on the right.

“Since your Mom’s diagnosis?” Ava said.

“Five years ago. My wound had healed and I was scheduled to report back to duty. But then, Mom called with her diagnosis. That’s why I was stateside when Josh...”

He continued to talk, but his words faded into the hum of the engine and the persistent click of the signal light.

“But you... were his commanding officer.”

He parked adjacent to her house. Hope yawned and scrambled out with the boys.

“I didn’t want to leave my unit, but I had to come home to be with Mom. I was replaced. Michelle came in to handle operational intel.”

Ava cradled the casserole Stella had sent home with her. “I see. Thanks for asking us to dinner. My family and I... we all needed the down time.”

With trembling fingers she smoothed the edge of the aluminum foil against the glass dish. The SUV rocked with her sons’ exits and a door clicked closed. After a steadying breath, she stepped onto the baked earth of the lane. The solid surface beneath her feet grounded her. All this time, she’d blamed Ryan for Josh’s death, and Michelle Frost had been in charge. Josh was one of the lost Marines who haunted Michelle’s dreams.

“Let me get that for you.” Ryan took the casserole from her.

Inside the security of her kitchen, Ava straightened. “Tomorrow I’ll try to have dinner on the table by five.” Thank goodness her voice didn’t reveal her inner turmoil. “But since there’s no school, our schedule may vary depending on our work.”

He stopped to open the front door. "We can hit pause until Monday."

She shook her head. "No. Business as usual."

After a pause he slid the casserole onto the kitchen counter. "Keeping tabs on my progress?"

"Absolutely." Too bad her words trembled like her fingers. "Your family was a gift." She itched to touch his cheek, rub her fingertips against the rasp of his stubble. Instead, she bunched his shirt sleeves in her hands. "You gave that to us."

"They deserve a chance to be boys." He took her hands in his and kissed her knuckles. "Just like you deserve a chance to be a woman."

"Today, that possibility didn't seem so distant."

He tilted his head. "Is there a *but* coming?"

His humor eased the pressure of building tears. "Don't give up on us." *On me.*

"No, ma'am." His low voice stroked her.

She moistened her lips. Life had taught her tomorrow was never guaranteed. If she thought it, she should say it. "Ryan."

His gaze held hers.

"Today, with you, your family, and friends, I felt ..." She wanted to drop her gaze, take a moment to regroup and find her way. But she couldn't.

She sucked in a deep breath. "When we lost Mom and Josh, we struggled and moved forward. But we couldn't fill a missing piece. Today that gap narrowed."

"I understand." He moved closer, his voice serious. "More than you know."

"Then we both healed a little."

He was staring at her mouth. In her house. With her children milling around. She stepped back.

His lip twitched. "Are you working this evening?"

Although the man could twist her tighter than a child's

windup toy, he'd have to be more careful in her home. "Do you ever get tired of being right?"

He winked. "No ma'am. I might even stop by later to see how my competition is doing."

"You won't recognize our site. We used to call it the Trash Place, but it's shaping up into a respectable commercial site."

A shadow clouded his smile, then disappeared. "Are you pressuring me?"

"Is it working?"

"Yes ma'am." He saluted. "Any chance we can move up our dinner date?"

She wished. "Are you worried the celebration will be for us? And by the way, I expect a private room with balloons and streamers."

"I'll need to find a different restaurant."

"Make sure it's a nice one." She put the casserole in the refrigerator. "I plan to win big."

"We could go out to dinner and still celebrate a victory."

She checked the hallway, and then wagged her finger at him. "You never quit."

"Some things are worth fighting for. There's a ballgame Tuesday night. We could call a cease fire. By that time we'll be closing in on the end."

He was staring again.

"My children are down the hall," she whispered.

His smile was pure heat. "Good argument for why we should take a break, Tuesday night. You and me."

The corner of his mouth lifted. He was so darned sure of himself—and her. "Okay. Tuesday night."

"I'll pick you up at six-thirty."

The man didn't have the decency to even act surprised. She let him get to the door. "And Ryan?"

He turned.

"You'll still owe me a big victory party."

CHAPTER SEVENTEEN

FINALLY, AN EVENING ALONE.

Tuesday evening, Ryan flipped through the hangers until his fingers landed on his favorite Hawaiian shirt. He moved on. Typical North Carolina fall had switched from warm and balmy to cold and dreary. Toward the back, the soft flannel in muted orange and red plaid brushed his fingers. Since when did he select clothes to match the season? He was one sorry Marine.

At precisely nineteen hundred hours, he turned onto Ava's rutted lane. The soft click of the SUV door blended with the chirps of the evening peepers. He shook out his hands, but the tingling continued.

As he climbed the steps, Hope's face appeared at the front door.

"Hey," Ryan said.

The little girl grabbed his hand and led him inside. The minute her velvety fingers touched him, the air rushed from his lungs. She giggled and took off down the hall, but the tinkle of her laughter chased around a crazy thought in his head. The Robey home calmed him. How had that happened?

He'd laid out his life plan ten years ago. It included a full ride in the military, win the competition for his Colonel, and help the Robey family. He'd made no plans for a family—this family.

A movement jarred him back to his surroundings. Although the TV blared, Nate was staring at him instead of the block figures on the screen. Ryan ran his hand along the window trim, pretending to check the cut. Nate narrowed his eyes. The kid wasn't buying his interest in wood. However, the youngest Robey male wouldn't press the issue without backup from his brothers.

"Where's the rest of the unit?" Ryan said.

"Talley's mom gave them a ride to the game."

"So, you have date night with Hope and I have date night with your mother?" The minute the words left his mouth, Ryan fisted his hand. He needed to hit the pause button, take a walk, clear his head. It wasn't every day a man realized his life had changed.

It didn't seem possible for a kid, but Nate's eyes had hardened. Becky Smith's dad had given him the same look the night he picked her up for his senior homecoming dance—over fifteen years ago.

Ava glided into the room. "Sorry, I'm late."

Ryan sucked in a breath. Gorgeous woman. He'd burn the coveralls that had hidden her legs—right after he ran his hand along the curve of her neck, the swell of her breasts, and the flare of her hips. Man, he didn't want to think about what was hidden beneath her soft orange dress.

"Are you ready?"

Heat scorched his ears. Ready? Was she kidding? "You bet."

Ava nudged his waist and he collided with Nate's narrowed glare, again. The kid had witnessed him almost panting over his mother. His luck, Nate would hold that over him for the rest of his life.

Outside, he opened the SUV door for Ava and held her hand to steady her climb into the seat. Warmed by the touch of her palm, the words *rest of his life* revolved in his head.

"You're quiet," she said. "Is something wrong?"

He buckled his seatbelt. His survival instinct screamed, hands two and four, eyes straight ahead. He turned to her. "Unbelievable," he said, soft as a prayer.

"What?"

He forced his mouth upward, but guessed the smile fell short. A furrow still lined her brow. "You." He hated the thickness in his tongue. "The dress, your hair—" He closed his mouth before another stupid remark rolled off his tongue.

When she cocked her head, a wisp of hair teased her right cheek. "Thank you. It felt strange dressing up."

Strange had been tilting his world since she'd entered it. "There's this place on the beach that serves the best mullet on the coast. I wanted to take you there. You know, like a real date?"

He turned around by her barn and eased the SUV toward the main road. His nose tickled. She smelled nice too. Dude, he was toast. "Anyway, when you said you didn't like to be far from the kids, I thought of something else."

"Thanks. I appreciate your understanding. The boys are usually responsible, but stuff happens."

Ten minutes later, he turned into his driveway. "I hope a nice meal at home is okay."

When she didn't protest, he figured he was in the clear and killed the engine. He hustled around the vehicle, but she'd already opened the door. Instead of holding out his hand, he grabbed her by the waist and lifted her down. Her eyes widened, and her mouth made an *O* of surprise. Flecks of gold and green sparkled in her eyes. When her feet touched the pavement, his hands lingered at her waist.

"No matter what we do, it will be perfect." The tooth with the slight flaw reflected the glow from the streetlight. "Mom is off-duty."

"I hope you're hungry. I'm starving." For her, but it was better than stuttering over an answer. He hoped she liked his efforts.

The ambiance he'd created worked best in the dark, so he didn't switch on the foyer light upon entry. Using the glow from the back porch, he led her to the family room. Through the bank of windows, the small twinkling lights he'd strung along the porch beams, the white tablecloth, and the fire from the pit, came into view. He held his breath.

The whisper of a gasp filled the silence.

"It's okay?" His question sounded more like the bullfrogs he used to catch as a boy.

"It's perfect."

"If you get an urgent call, I can get you home in three-point-five minutes."

She laughed, the clear, throaty sound filling the silence. "That too."

He held open the back door for her. "My chef skills are limited, so it's steaks again. But I bought real lettuce and chopped it this time."

"Upping your game?" She tilted her head to one side.

"Whatever it takes to keep you coming back."

"A woman likes to be pampered. I've never had a man who cooks. Grilled, yes. But a guy who plans and prepares the entire meal? This is a first."

"I've never had a woman with tools, so there you go." Except they weren't going anywhere. At least he wasn't. Ava had rooted his shoes to the floor.

A timer chimed in the distance. "I turned the oven down

before I left, but our baked potatoes may taste more like dried turds."

"Bon appétit." She grinned. "My boys would love the visual."

"Too many meals with men." Well, hell. He was a Marine, not a banker. "There's a bottle of red on the counter. Want a glass while I grill the steaks?"

"Please. But one's my limit. I need to keep my wits about me."

She was messing with him—without even trying. One glance, a twist of words, or her low throaty laugh, and she reduced him to a teenager.

While she settled in a chair by the fire pit, he forked the steaks on the grill with a sizzle. The aroma of seasoned beef and charcoal peppered the air and stirred his appetite. In the firelight's glow, Ava's dark hair reflected the embers like the sparks in her eyes. Another appetite surged to the surface. He didn't have a taste for wine, but he had a taste for her.

With a shove of the tongs, he turned the steaks. The fire hissed. He loved a good piece of meat, cooked crispy on the outside with a hot tender center, but his gaze kept wandering to Ava. He couldn't seem to control the desire to be at her side. Which didn't make sense. He'd been with women. A few had been knock-dead gorgeous. But not one had turned his brains to sand like Ava.

When he plated the steaks, her soft gaze captured his. Amazing woman and amazing he managed to get the food to the table without dropping it on the patio.

"So," Ava cut a bite-sized piece of beef. "You've made your mark in the Afghan mountains. You're respected in your field. Where to next?"

A life with you. He chased a bite of steak down with a drink of wine. The quiet of the night, the satisfaction of the meal, the crack of the fire, eased the tightness in his shoulders. He wiped his mouth on his napkin.

"I like my work at Lejeune. It's close to home, but I'll be reassigned in a few years."

"I don't miss that part of military life."

"The Corps is like a woman. You must woo her to give you what you need. Of course, all things come at a price."

"Really?"

He laughed and lifted his glass to her. "There's politics in every aspect of life. The Corps is no different. Sunberry is my home, but the Corps doesn't care. They let me come home to help out."

She wrinkled her nose. "Did that cost you?"

"Yes ma'am. The Corps wants one hundred percent. They don't like bumps. Makes them think a man isn't committed."

"Slow down a promotion?"

He didn't know why her accurate guess surprised him. As a Marine wife, she knew the ropes.

"I got passed over the first time around. I've been trying to make up for the deviation." He shrugged off the sudden surge of frustration. This was her night and he didn't want his professional goals to dominate the conversation. He also didn't want to make a choice between Ava and the Corps. But it was happening and he couldn't stop it.

"You're good with men and boys."

He suppressed the sudden urge to pump up his chest. "That's what I've been trained to do."

"It's more than training," she said. "It's like teachers. They're all trained to educate, but some have a special talent. Hope's kindergarten teacher is a natural. All the kids love her, and they want to learn."

"I wouldn't say my men love me."

"They respect you. You can see it."

He hoped she couldn't see the impact her praise had on him. "It's important to prepare men before deployment."

"So, you're going for the full ride until retirement?"

"I don't know." His mouth dried.

Her brows disappeared under her hair. "The guy who has a plan to cut his toenails doesn't know his career path?"

"I don't have a toenail plan."

"Sure you do. I'll bet the first weekend of the month."

"There's nothing wrong with a hygiene schedule."

She wagged her index finger at him. "I can't believe it. I'm right."

The harder he shook his head, the more she giggled. She had the funniest laugh—kind of a cross between a hiccup and a snort. A laugh exploded from him and took the indecision with it. She eased the angst, soothed him, made him feel good—like life would work out.

She sobered. "You've got an amazing smile. You should use it more."

"I will if it works with you."

"Laughter works for whatever ails you."

"It makes me feel better," he said. "But it doesn't work for the Board. They review my record and decide to bump me up."

She wrinkled her nose. "And you want the full ride?"

"If things fall into place."

"So, if you get passed over, you continue to do what you love doing." She forked a piece of steak into her mouth.

He shook his head. "No, I retire."

"Oh. Sorry. I didn't mean to minimize the situation. I was trying to cheer you up."

He reached across the table and covered her small hand with his, marveling at the delicate bones beneath his fingers. She raised her chin, her gaze soft, caring.

"You do more than cheer me up." His voice sounded rusty.

"You're like a star in a midnight sky—a shining light that fills my mind with wonder."

She blinked. "Men don't say things like that."

"You're right." Heat raced up his face. "It's downright embarrassing."

She got up, walked up behind him, and kissed his cheek. His chest swelled. This amazing woman liked him despite the stupid crap coming from his mouth.

"The Corps would be crazy to let you go," she murmured.

He'd be crazier to let *her* go.

She winked and returned to her seat. "You seem like a man who succeeds."

"Sometimes."

She didn't look away.

He halted the involuntary bobbing of his chin. "I'd like to succeed with you." Holy crap, he was pathetic.

She stared over the rim of her glass. "Describe success."

Making her dream come true without letting down Schmidt. Spending time with her without thinking about the blasted competition, his investment plan for the parking and retail space. She was relaxed, smiling, flirting. She deserved a break and so did he. They shared dinner and reported every night—every night but tonight. So when should he tell her? When did he risk her anger?

Pink juice oozed from his steak, so he went for chewing in place of running his mouth. He'd negotiate a business deal with her tomorrow. Negotiate? Not in her vocabulary. Ava didn't negotiate terms, she spit fire and he got into line. His lip twitched. He could go for fire in the bedroom. When he looked up, her gaze had dropped to her plate. He swallowed.

"I'm a simple man. I'd say success is an evening alone with you. Sharing a meal. Sharing dreams." Her look grilled him darker than the steak. He gulped his wine. "Is the steak okay? I can cook it longer if you like."

She cut a small piece and nipped it off her fork. He blinked. She chewed and smiled. Maybe he hadn't screwed it up. Women were so complex. He didn't know you could do that—chew and smile. Right now, he struggled with breathing and watching her.

He poured more wine in his glass, but hers remained untouched. She'd said one. But he needed to do something with his hands that didn't include sharp utensils. "Did you finish the furniture scene you were working on?"

She shoved at a wispy dark tendril near her right eye. "Haven't had time."

"When's your projected open date?"

She sipped her wine, but her gaze had narrowed on him. "Stop worrying about the competition."

When he won, she'd need a new plan—with him. But he didn't want to fight her. He wanted to love her. Maybe tomorrow at dinner. Better yet, after dinner on a walk around the pond. They'd have privacy.

When she stacked her utensils on top of her plate fifteen minutes later, he stood. "I'll get these. Sit by the fire. Relax."

She smiled and he fumbled the silverware.

"Can I refresh your glass, or would you prefer something else? I have coffee, hot chocolate?" He was making a fool of himself.

"Mm, hot chocolate sounds yummy."

"And safe," he added.

After placing the stack of dirty dishes on the counter, he turned. One day he'd learn she didn't follow his orders. She stood behind him, her cheeks rosy and her bedroom eyes—Whoa. When did he think of her with bedroom eyes?

"No cleaning," he said in a strained tone. "Since I couldn't take you out, at least let me wait on you."

She tilted her face upward, all traces of humor gone from her gaze.

"You amaze me, Ava Robey." So much for finesse, but with her golden eyes beckoning him, he couldn't seem to control his tongue.

"How so?" she murmured, her smoky voice racing through his system like warm coffee on a cold night.

"Just like that. Every time I think I've got a bead on you, you surprise me. You're a target I can't track. You confuse me." He stroked along her arms. "Seduce me."

When her chest lifted, his hands drifted lower, seeking to touch her breasts. Her gaze held him captivated. "You're a beautiful woman," he managed before kissing her.

When he touched the seam of her lips with his tongue, she accepted him. The taste of wine and the warm recesses of her mouth sucked him deeper. *Slow down.* He wasn't an out-of-control teen. Love her, respect her for the beautiful woman she was.

With the moonlight filtering through the window, Ava cast in silhouette filled his mind. Her milky skin, glittery eyes, and dark hair blurred his vision, spun the room around them.

Although shaky with desire, he stepped back and held out his hand for her. "Are you sure?"

She rested her fingertips on his, the lightest of touches, and nodded. "Yes, Ryan. I want you."

He didn't hesitate. A Marine *always* followed orders.

CHAPTER EIGHTEEN

Ava had gone too long without sex. Content in Ryan's bed, she nestled her back against Ryan's coarse chest hairs. "You better have an awesome dessert planned."

The sudden stillness behind her made her grin. He rolled her to face him.

Despite the darkness of the room, his white teeth flashed. "Just what a man wants to hear after making love to a woman."

Made love not sex. Her flesh cooled. Was she ready for love? Talk about engaging in risky business—especially for her. As for her body? The wink had pretty much done it for her.

She tugged at his chest hair.

"Ow!" He grabbed at her wrist, but she rolled away.

"Can't let you get too cocky after I submitted to your advances." She placed her hands on her hips. "Just because we didn't go out to eat, doesn't mean you're off the hook for dessert."

Ryan stood. Wide shoulders tapering into a long torso and... Her breath hitched and then escaped in a hiccup.

She stepped back, holding up her palm. "Wipe that lustful gleam from your eyes. You're not getting back inside this body until I've had dessert."

His gaze roved from the tips of her unpainted toes to her hair, which probably looked like last year's bird nest. He must be into bird nests. Too bad, she wasn't into thinking. When he looked at her like that, thinking tanked.

He grabbed her by the wrist and moved toward the kitchen.

"Ryan!"

"You wanted dessert," he said. "We're having dessert."

With his long stride, she had to trot to keep up.

"I... don't eat... naked."

When he glanced back, she understood how the bunnies felt right before Toby took up a chase. Ryan looked like he could gobble her in one sexy bite. She froze, but he caught her misstep, his hand gliding from her hip to beneath her right breast.

"Ryan," she whispered.

Dark hooded eyes studied her. Nothing wrong with the man's libido. Nothing wrong with floating in bliss. Something she hadn't experienced since she'd lost Josh.

He drew in a ragged breath and dropped his hand. Without warning he scooped her into his arms and deposited her on the kitchen stool.

"This isn't sanitary," she said in a hoarse whisper.

"Neither am I." He mimicked her hushed response. "Don't push your luck because I've got a kinky idea about dessert floating around up here." He touched his forehead.

When he moved to the pantry, she picked up a dish towel. The little rectangle wouldn't hide anything, but twisting it into a tight knot kept her hands out of trouble.

Ryan set a box of graham crackers and a bag of marshmallows on the counter beside her and then added a chocolate bar. Although his gaze burned her with a dangerous intensity, his lips brushed hers with a feather-lite touch.

He planted his hands on both sides of her and leaned close. “Not once in two weeks have you served dessert, so I wasn’t prepared.”

His gaze lowered, and he brushed her shoulder with a kiss before returning to hold her gaze. “It’s too cold for ice cream. How do you feel about s’mores?”

Right now, she was hungrier for him, but she’d wanted distance. Food met the criteria.

“Chocolate and peanut butter?” she said. “What’s not to like?”

His brows did the caterpillar thing across the bridge of his nose. “S’mores don’t include peanut butter.”

“Of course they do.”

“No, ma’am. I was in the scouts. Chocolate, marshmallows, and graham crackers are the key ingredients.”

Who knew an old family tradition would provide a needed distraction? “Robey S’mores include peanut butter and sliced almonds, if you have them.”

Ryan lifted his palms. “I’m a Marine, not a chef.”

“No sliced almonds? What about peanut butter?”

He opened a pack of crackers on a dish and handed her a knife. “Every Marine has peanut butter. It’s an essential like duct tape.”

She saluted. His lip twitched one moment before he disappeared inside the pantry.

He thrust a family-sized jar at her. “You spread. I’ll toast marshmallows.”

It was only a peek and one couldn’t fault a gal for looking. However, leave it to a Marine to catch her lustful glance down the naked length of him.

Pure heat tainted his smile. “Hold that thought.”

Thoughts? She pressed too hard on the knife and broke

the first cracker. A mother of four did not spread peanut butter butt-naked at a man's counter. Her cheeks were hot enough to toast the marshmallows. But she was not backing away from Ryan. Worse, the nutty smell reminded her of Hope. So not a good thought considering her actions.

Before she'd covered four crackers, he returned dressed in red flannel sleep pants. "I hate to see you cover up." He handed a matching shirt to her. "But all that flesh is dangerous, especially around the fireplace."

Dangerous didn't begin to describe the thoughts swimming in her mind. She shrugged into his shirt and then spread peanut butter like it was a life or death race. After a quick glance toward the living room to ensure he wasn't looking, she dumped the three broken crackers in the trash. Where was Toby when she needed him?

At least her task kept her focused on something besides the pounding of blood in her ears. Since Ryan had his back to her roasting the marshmallows, she took three cleansing breaths that didn't do squat to stop the swimming in her head.

"Okay, Ava," she mouthed. "Behave." But how did a woman control her sexual urges with a man like Ryan highlighted in the fire's glow?

"Yummy," she said.

"Perfect timing." He pushed four golden brown marshmallows onto her crackers.

After quick and somewhat erratic construction, she bit into her s'more and let the warm chocolate mixture explode on her tongue. Her ears buzzed from the sugar high or more likely a Ryan high.

She licked her sticky fingers. "From now on I'm adding dessert to my meals."

He captured a bubble of marshmallow from the side of her lip with his thumb. "I was hoping you'd add me."

She froze searching his features for meaning—almost afraid to contemplate his suggestion.

"Too much too soon?" He lifted his hands. "No pressure. You've got a lot on your plate. A lot to consider."

The dessert plates cleaned much easier than the possibilities roaming in her head. After the quick cleanup, he snuggled her against him on the corduroy sofa. Across from them, the blue and orange flame crackled and threw undulating light patterns around the silent room.

She nestled closer, the warmth of his cheek near her head comforting her. "This is nice."

His chuckle rumbled like her old lawn mower.

"What?"

"I was thinking about your family." He rubbed a big hand along her arm. "Hope's like a miniature you. She could wrap the most calloused Marine around her little finger. The boys may give you fits, but they'll get through teen years and grow into fine men. They possess an amazing work ethic for teens and they hang together. They're a unit and it's because of you."

Unexpected tears filled her eyes. "They are, aren't they?"

His nod slid along her hair. "How'd you do it?"

Her story after Josh died surfaced raw and primal. But she demanded honesty from her family and Ryan. Secrets destroyed relationships and although unplanned, she'd entered a relationship with this man.

"I can't take the credit. My boys survived trial by fire."

When a shiver shook her shoulders, he tightened his embrace. "You don't have to explain your past to me. A few holes here and there aren't going to scare me off."

But it was time. Maybe she needed to say the words, too. "The boys never talk about that time and Hope was too little to remember it. Josh's death destroyed me."

When she paused, Ryan opened his palm to her. Still shaky, she placed her hand on his.

"After his death, I couldn't get out of bed. Couldn't stand to look at my devastated boys. I couldn't take their hurt away." She shook her head, but Kyle, Whit, and Nate's faces filled her mind. "I kept thinking, it's not going to get better. That's the scariest part. Everything hurts inside and out and it's not going to stop.

While I was nearly incapacitated, my boys, barely out of elementary school, carried on. Kyle got everyone up, and dressed Hope every morning. Nate made beds and picked up the dirty clothes. Whit took over cooking. He had to stand on a stool at the counter, but we had scrambled eggs, pancakes, and peanut butter sandwiches."

Although the words had spilled from her, she couldn't draw in enough air. Behind her, Ryan remained stone still, except for his long fingers. His thumb had started the familiar circle on the back of her palm.

"That's why I have to stay strong. My boys pulled me through it. They lost a dad. They deserve a strong mother. A mother they can rely on."

He kissed her temple. "Thanks for telling me."

She straightened so she could see his features. "I don't want sympathy. But if we're moving forward, you need to understand about me and my family."

He nodded, his gaze never leaving her.

"I moved us back to Sunberry, but I hadn't moved on. I was too dependent on Josh. When I lost him, I lost my way." She studied him, watching for a challenge. "That's why I cherish my independence. Life is tentative. I'm never going back to that dependent widow. I'm never going to set me and my family up to experience that again. Never."

Ryan pulled her back against his chest and circled her with long, corded arms. "Life doesn't come with guarantees.

That's why you grab every good thing that comes your way like it's your last gift."

The pressure pushing from all sides of her eased. Exhausted, she rested her head against his shoulder. She'd take his gift of understanding, absorb his tenderness, his compassion, and his support.

"Losing people you love is hard." Ryan paused between words like he was selecting the ones to touch her heart. "Connections are important. My family, my buddies... you, have helped me fill the loss in my life."

"Me?"

He kissed her forehead, barely grazing her flesh and then turned and kissed her brow, her tear-stained cheeks, the corner of her mouth.

"You," he whispered. "I think I'm falling in love with you."

Her breath eased past her lips, but she didn't speak the words he probably wanted and expected to hear. For now, she'd accept his gift and his words of wisdom. Maybe—in the future—once she'd opened Robey's Rewards, she'd untangle her feelings for Ryan. But the opening had to come first. Like he said, life didn't offer guarantees.

CHAPTER NINETEEN

AVA MIGHT BE COMING AROUND, BUT MOTHER NATURE WAS dead set against him.

Wednesday morning, rain hammered Eastern Carolina. Ryan drummed his fingers against the steering wheel. In front of his vehicle, the concrete truck idled. The curtain of rain clouded the forms for the new sidewalk and drive he'd built yesterday afternoon. Everything had fallen into place right on schedule—until today. Although he'd despised beating Ava, he'd never planned on losing.

The driver beeped and left. One more nail in his coffin. However, Ava and her boys were still laying tile. If the front moved out, he might still pull the rabbit out of the hat and win. Winning the competition wouldn't help him with the funding the banker had denied. His big win-win plan to develop retail and a parking garage across from the Opera House was circling the drain. It seems his banker buddy wasn't willing to take a gamble on an active duty Marine.

Fifteen minutes later, Ryan paced his kitchen. When he jerked open the refrigerator door, Hope's blue box drawing drifted to the floor. The smiley face and the irregular print eased the tension bunching the back of his neck.

When his cell phone chimed, Schmidt's name filled the screen.

"Did you pour?"

The storm must be interfering with the signal.

"Seriously?" Ryan scrubbed the frustration from his voice. "It's not letting up. The rain will contaminate the mix."

"Lana packed up this morning." The shaky quality to Schmidt's voice had nothing to do with the transmission. "She's going to stay with her sister in Wilmington for a while."

Just what they didn't need—escalation. "Sorry to hear that. But we're not washed out yet." Ryan gave a status on the competition. "The Sunberry lease isn't what you need. Lease a site near the Wilmington Riverwalk. It's a bigger city with more traffic—"

"Lana likes Sunberry!"

"Hey, Marine. Stand down. It's you and me. We can work this out."

"Her kid came in drunk last night," Schmidt whispered.

Ryan checked the screen. If Lana had left, why was Schmidt whispering?

"Schmidt, do you need me to come over? I'm at home. I can be there—"

"Just win the competition!"

"I can't control the weather. The forms are covered. But we can't pour in a monsoon. So right now, winning depends on our opposition. But even if this crap lets up, it'll be a horse race to the wire. You need to talk to Lana, anyway. Bring up the Riverwalk idea."

"Derrick woke me out of a deep sleep. I reacted."

Shit! Ryan gripped the phone. "Is he okay?"

Stories about disoriented Marines overreacting to external

stimuli made the rounds. None were good news. That's why the military handed out family safety tips. Marines returning from deployment were hypervigilant. It took time to acclimate to a safe environment.

"I didn't pull the trigger," Schmidt whispered. "But Lana went rabid."

"Is Derrick okay?"

"The kid was too drunk to notice."

Ryan swallowed. "Have you seen anyone yet?"

"You sound like Lana. I'll get this under control. It's taking longer this time and my stepson isn't helping."

"Listen, Schmidt, I can help you with this. I'll set up the appointment. Go with you, drive you, whatever you need. You are not alone—"

"No. I'm good. Just win the lease. I need to show her I'm moving in the right direction."

Right direction? Ryan scrubbed his hand over his head. He had to turn this around. "You and Lana need good news now. We won't know the competition outcome until tomorrow, maybe the next day. We can't guarantee we'll win. If we find a Wilmington site, you can give her good news. I'll look with—"

"It's got to be Sunberry. Okay? Sunberry."

"I got it." Ryan replaced Hope's picture beneath the magnet. "I'm coming over. We can talk—"

"No! I don't need talk. I need action. I'm depending on you. Don't let me down."

"I'm coming over. Your weapons go in my gun safe or I escalate this incident."

"That's not necessary—"

"Your choice."

The refrigerator hummed. Outside, rain rushed through the gutters. Ryan checked the screen. Still connected. Schmidt was one hard-headed Marine.

"Major?"

"Right here." He traced Hope's box. She'd stayed in the lines but still needed help on her letters. A gap broke the bar connecting the parallel lines of her H.

"I'll bring them to you in thirty minutes."

When the call disconnected, Ryan leaned against the cool stainless-steel surface. Instead of finishing concrete, he needed to develop a method to eliminate Marine stubbornness. Better yet, a way to give two deserving families a single lease.

Get it together, Marine. He set his phone timer for twenty-nine minutes. If Schmidt didn't pull into his drive with his firearms, he was driving to the Colonel's house to collect them. A cold sweat formed along his hairline. If he convinced Butler to partner with him on the parking garage, Ava and Schmidt could accomplish their mission—if Ryan retired. Ava wouldn't like it. He'd just have to convince her his decision was in his best interest. Yeah, and that would piss her off big time. If he wanted a chance with her.

Ryan paced to the fireplace, turned, marched to the kitchen, and repeated the route. When he passed the mantle, the light from the kitchen reflected on the frame of Robey's photo. Three Marines in front of an armored jeep. They'd even smiled for the photo. Ryan straightened the frame and something scraped against the wood. When he lifted the photo, a small dark outline broke the line between the wall and the mantle—Robey's rock.

Outside, a limb banged against the front window. The rock slipped from his fingers.

When he bent to retrieve the stone, thunder shattered the silence. His vision fogged. *Don't let go*. His sergeant's order increased in volume and then faded with the remembered whop, whop, whop of chopper blades. The rock rippled beneath the pads of his fingers. Ryan wiped the sweat tickling his face with his shoulder. On Memory Night Kyle had slapped his rock against the table.

Ryan blinked. Robey had scratched each boy's initial on the stone. W for Whit. N for Nate, and a K for cantankerous Kyle. Except he thought cantankerous started with the letter C. Hope had used the tattered toy. He'd considered buying a new stuffed animal for her, but a father's gift couldn't be replaced.

Robey should've carved a stone for Hope. Ryan froze, his ragged breaths echoing in the quiet. Parallel lines. The whop of helicopter blades, the sting of sand, and the metallic taste of blood. He swallowed, his mouth bone dry.

His Sergeant had given him the rock for focus, a focus to save his life. Before that night, before he'd gone down, the rock had another purpose. Robey probably thought he had enough time to find another stone for Hope. He hadn't. But Ryan could. He might fail Ava and Schmidt, but he wouldn't fail Hope.

THAT EVENING FOR DINNER, Kyle met him at the front door. "Did you finish the concrete work?"

Ryan shook out his hands from the rainy sprint to the house. "You're a regular comedian."

"Not me." The kid grinned. "Not an ounce of humor runs in these veins. I'm just scouting the competition."

Despite his aggravation with Schmidt, the weather and his banker, Ryan suppressed a grin. The teen couldn't wait to celebrate, but he was also cautious, smart.

"What about tomorrow?"

Ryan removed his boots and entered the house in his sock feet. "Concrete takes a while to cure. If I'm careful, I can remove the forms tomorrow evening."

"Yes!" Kyle pumped his fist. "We'll be finished tomorrow afternoon. But good try."

Yeah, right. The boys had worked hard. They deserved some room to crow about their accomplishments. In the meantime, he needed to find Ava, inhale her woman's scent, drag his hands down her warm flesh—and jump out of a plane without a chute. Geez, he had enough problems without creating more. Ryan followed a spicy aroma coming from the kitchen and found Ava in front of the oven.

"Dinner will be ready in twenty minutes. Bennie brought me a mess of fish. I hope rice and fish are okay?"

He rammed his hands into his pockets to keep from touching her. "Sure."

"How'd it go today?"

Better now that he was with her. She glanced over her shoulder and his heart pummeled his ribs. Since four chaperones hovered in the next room, he reported his lack of progress. Unlike her son, she didn't celebrate his defeat. With a graceful movement, she moved to the right and lined biscuits on a pan to warm.

"I'm sorry. This isn't how I wanted to win."

"A beautiful woman warned me she didn't tolerate slackers." But he was counting on her to ease the knots in his gut.

She winked. "Harsh woman."

So much for knots. "I keep reliving our night together," he whispered.

She mouthed the word "children."

"Just saying," but the sparkle in her eye told him she'd been reliving those vivid memories too. "If dinner's not for another twenty minutes, we have time for a private talk on the porch."

She set a timer on her phone and slipped it into her hip pocket—right over that fine backside. As if he needed additional frustration for the day.

He snatched an afghan from the sofa back and followed her to the swing. That first day with Ava, he'd doubted the antique could support his weight. He'd harbored lots of doubts that day. Most hadn't materialized, especially the ones about Ava and her family.

"Hello?" The musical quality of her voice blended with the rain pelting the roof. "Where are you?"

He pulled her close to his side and her contented sigh awakened places that needed to sleep. He straightened his legs and pushed. The chain creaked.

"I was thinking about the first time I sat here with you." The fresh scent of her hair eased the thud behind his right eye. "I thought you needed a Marine to help you out. Looks like I'm the one who needs the help."

"What are you going to do when you lose?"

"Until this morning losing hadn't been a consideration."

"If it's any help, I'm really excited about opening my shop."

"I'm happy for you. But I let the Colonel down," he said. "What was your plan if you lost?"

She settled against him. "No negative vibes in the Robey house."

After a quick check for prying eyes, he brushed a kiss to her hair.

"I made a promise to think positive. I focused on winning just like you." Her timer vibrated. "I better get back. Hungry natives get very irritable."

Damn, he needed more time. Grinding his molars, he followed her to the kitchen. "How far along are you with the tile?"

"If school were out, we'd finish by noon. By myself—" She scrunched her face. "I'll finish the hallway. The boys arrive at 3:30— Probably 5:30 or 6:00."

She moistened her lips with her tongue and his thoughts headed south. “Have you heard from Colonel Schmidt?”

He coughed. “I talked to him today. He’s...upset.” Nothing like minimizing Schmidt’s meltdown.

“I hope that means he’s getting help.”

“I wouldn’t count on it. He’s a proud man.” Sweat formed in his hairline and oozed along his jaw. “Ava—”

“There’s no shame in getting help.” She stirred the rice in the skillet. “Did you?”

Despite the spicy aroma filling the kitchen, his stomach churned like he was coming down with a bug.

“Some of us make it through the other side—especially those with strong family ties.” He glanced toward the living room where the boys argued about some unknown topic. He needed privacy, but he couldn’t pull her away from dinner. Besides, her sons ate like they’d never get another meal so a delay would ensure interruption.

The clink of metal on glass sounded louder than usual.

Ava’s mouth tightened and her brow wrinkled. Navigating a woman had never been one of his talents, but the back of his neck kept itching like he’d stepped on an IED with a delayed trigger. Her eyes narrowed. If he gave her a few details, maybe she’d smile again.

“I was hypervigilant at first. Sudden, loud sounds bothered me. But I got over it. Now, it’s my job to help other Marines.” A job more frustrating than trying to fill a rathole with sand.

Although she continued to prepare the meal without comment, the loud pops and scrapes diminished so he figured he’d appeased her—for now. But he still had to get through to Schmidt. He hoped Ava might have a few ideas. Plus, he’d like to talk to her about next steps—now that she’d accomplished her dream.

He checked the kitchen window. “Looks like the clouds

are breaking up. Can we walk around the pond after dinner?" Every time he thought about his *great* plan, it sounded worse.

She spooned the steaming meal into a serving bowl. "I'd like that."

Five minutes after they'd settled around the dinner table, his phone signaled.

"Sorry." He removed his phone from his waist clip. "I need to take this."

Crap, he couldn't catch a break today. Talk about timing. Schmidt continued in a booming voice that almost shattered Ryan's eardrums.

"Hold on, sir." But Schmidt kept yammering. Ryan pushed away from the table and hurried to the porch. Based on stares coming his way, the family got the gist of the conversation before his exit. Moments later he returned to the table, the amazing meal Ava had prepared curdling his stomach.

"Looks like we're busting it tonight." Kyle's voice had lost its usual bravado.

"Schmidt blew the water out of the forms and found a retired Marine to deliver concrete in twenty minutes." Ryan spit out each word like they were tiny bones in the fish meat.

When he shook his head, Ava dropped her utensils on her plate with a clatter. "So the real race is on?"

He opened his mouth and closed it. Words were insufficient and he couldn't fold her in his arms.

"Life happens. We've survived harder events than this." She lifted her chin and straightened. She stood tall. Not a broken widow, but with steel in her spine and sass in her tone.

The urge to hoist her on his shoulders and race around the yard with the dog yapping at his heels surged through him. Nothing knocked her down. That's why he needed to lift her up, stop tripping her up. He hated the situation, but he admired the way she met it head on. The bud of her lip teased him. He ran his tongue against his teeth. But he had no right to think about loving her. Had no right to beat her like this.

Smack! A sharp sting raced from the palms of his hand and the plates rattled. "I can't do this. You and the boys, even Hope, have worked so hard. I can't rip the win out of your fist at the last minute like this."

Hope jerked upright.

"Sorry, Hope." Ryan lowered his voice. "I'm not mad at you. Any of you. I'm mad at the situation."

"Okay," Hope murmured.

The ache in his head intensified.

Ava stood, her gaze on fire. "If it were Josh suffering from PTSD, would you let us win?"

"It's not the same."

"I think it is," she said. "We've worked our butts off. My boys came together like young men and proved their loyalty and love for this family. We're Robey strong. And no matter if we lease Main Street or decide to make a go with another location, we're successful because we did the work—as a family."

He forced his leaden muscles to stand. "It's been an honor and privilege to compete with you. Your father would be proud of the men you've become."

Unable to bear the boys' stunned looks, he turned and exited before he broke his pledge. He'd failed Ava and her family. He couldn't fail another Marine.

CHAPTER TWENTY

LOSING A COMPETITION COULDN'T COMPARE TO THE LOSS OF a father. Ava squared her shoulders and approached her stunned kids.

"Do not hang your heads in defeat. I am proud of the work you've done, and you should feel the same pride. We may lose a competition, but we have one another. We have our health. So wipe those sad looks off your faces and give me a hug."

Kyle hung back. "If we work all night, we can finish."

She moved Hope aside and cupped Kyle's bristled jaw in her palm. He'd leave to start his own life soon.

"School day, tomorrow. Regular night. We'll work until eight-thirty and stop."

His eyes narrowed with the same stubborn streak burning inside her. "And then what? You go back to work alone?" He shook his head. "We started this task together. That's how we're ending it. Besides, I'm so far ahead of the class it's ridiculous."

Nate stood. "Me too."

"I can miss one day," Whit added.

Hope yawned. “I can help.”

“Well, I’m still in command.” She’d come a long way from the widow who couldn’t climb from her bed five years ago.

“I’m coming,” Kyle said. “We’re a family like you said. That means we work together.”

“That means I give the orders and all of you take them.” Except her order had lost its starch.

When she turned, Whit shook his head and his chin trembled. Her breath rushed from her lips. Everything came harder for her compassionate middle son. She didn’t want to exclude him, but he had enough trouble staying up with his peers. She couldn’t weaken.

“You have a test tomorrow. Don’t deny it.” She held his gaze. “Besides, it’s your turn to stay with Hope. We’ll be hungry in the morning. You can fix breakfast.”

“Mom—”

“That’s how you can help me,” she said. “In the meantime, I need you to make peanut butter sandwiches and load the cooler for tonight. Nate, Kyle change into work clothes.”

FOUR HOURS LATER, Ava pushed from her hands and knees and stretched. Almost midnight. They’d made good progress. She’d completed grouting the tile in the hallway. Only the main room remained. If they could maintain their pace, they’d finish by morning and possibly beat Ryan.

“Mom,” Nate called from the back. “We’ve got company.”

The hairs along her forearms lifted despite the film of dust covering her flesh. Nate pushed the back door open and Michelle Frost and Whit walked into the room.

“Now, Mom,” Whit started.

Michelle raised both hands. “At ease, Whit.”

Ava checked behind them. “Where’s Hope?”

“Home with Talley.” Michelle met her gaze, woman-to-woman. "We didn't follow the chain of command, but this is an emergency. Marines and their families have to act."

Ava stiffened. Except this was her family and she'd left instructions—

"Plus," Michelle's tone softened. "I need to help. Not because of what happened with your husband."

When Michelle swallowed, Ava's chest tightened. Seeking and accepting help was hard, especially for women. Even harder for a woman in Michelle's position. Ava squeezed her arm and nodded.

"I wanted you to know I didn't come here as an officer," Michelle said. "I came as a woman. Please. Let me do this for your family."

Although nothing made Ava feel better than to know she'd helped someone in need, she couldn't agree. "It's me and my boys against Ryan. Those are the terms."

"For the competition." Michelle cocked her head and a smirk lifted her full lips. "There's nothing in the agreement about helping with the home front, is there?"

"Nope." A half-chuckle slipped out. "Not a word, my new best friend Michelle. I like the way you think. When this is over, I'd like to buy you a cup of coffee."

"Make that a strong drink during women's happy hour and you've got a date."

Ava almost saluted before pivoting to face her middle son. Whit's hopeful look twisted her heart.

"Talley tutored me the entire evening," Whit said. "I'll pass my exam tomorrow. Promise."

And what kind of mother would take away his determination to help, to be a part of his family's commitment? She'd been wrong to refuse to his help the same way she'd been wrong to refuse Ryan's. The same as almost refusing Michelle. Ava released a ragged breath. A snarky grin twisted Kyle's lips. Nate's gaze darted from her to Kyle and then to Michelle. Whit shrugged.

Ava dropped her chin. "What about Hope?"

"Talley's spending the night at your place," Michelle said.

This time Ava didn't suppress her chuckle. Of course Michelle would be equipped with mom antenna.

"I'll pick up the boys in the morning. I'll drop Nate and Kyle off at home so they can get some sleep, and then take Whit and Hope to school. That will free you to visit Butler for your lease."

"If we win," Ava said.

"When we win," the boys said in unison.

Ava opened her mouth and closed it. She'd accept their help with gratitude. No more standing on her own. "That works for me."

"Hey, Bro." Kyle shoved Whit in the shoulder. "Did you come up with that plan?"

Whit looked down at the floor. "Talley helped."

"And I executed it," Michelle finished. "Team effort."

"The best team ever." Ava removed a wadded tissue from her pocket. "I accept your offer and your friendship. Thank you. All of you. Let's grout the tile!"

CHAPTER TWENTY-ONE

WHAT A MAN—HE'D BEAT AVA AND HER KIDS.

At o-nine hundred on Thursday morning, Ryan drove through Sunberry's historic district. Art Butler lived on a narrow street that curved through stately old homes set close to the sidewalks. Still darkened with moisture and stripped of the last fall leaves, skeletal branches reached to a blue sky.

In front of the third house on the right, he turned into the drive and cut off the engine. Last chance to complete his commitment to Schmidt and save Ava's dream. Bankers wouldn't risk loans to deployed Marines operating as absentee contractors, but if Butler would partner with a retired Marine, they could pull it off.

Grace Butler, with her crown of snowy curls, answered the door after the first ring. "Ryan? What a pleasant surprise. We're sitting down for breakfast. Please, join us."

"I'm pretty grubby. Would you ask Art to meet me out here?"

True to her southern roots, Gracie nodded. "I'll send him out. Coffee?"

"A cup would be great."

The proposal required fifteen minutes and fifteen pounds from Ryan's hide. But Butler agreed. Now, if Ryan could convince Ava to approve, maybe he could fix this nightmare.

Art shook his hand. "Here's to a successful partnership."

From the street, breaks squealed and Ava's rusted Explorer rolled to a stop. When their gazes locked and her smile faded, another pound of flesh melted from him. After a slight hesitation she squared her shoulders and marched to the round patio. Dark circles shadowed her eyes and lines creased the pretty mouth that had sassed him, pleasured him.

"I see I'm late," Ava said.

He clenched his jaw to keep from denying her claim and sheltering her in his arms. But she wouldn't want or accept his protection. With luck and a prayer, she might accept his proposal.

Art stood. "Ms. Robey, please, have a seat."

She shook her head making the limp hair that had worked free of her kerchief swing around her face.

"I'm too dirty. I wanted to be here at nine...in case..." Her chin trembled. "I knew it would be close. We worked all night hoping to finish before Ryan."

Art pulled out a chair. "Don't worry about a little dirt. I'm sorry you worked all night."

Ava accepted a glass of juice from Gracie. "Robeys don't stop until they cross the finish line."

"Close race," Art said. "I'm sorry about the competition. Me and Grace— We support our troops. When we received your lease offer the same time as Colonel Schmidt's, we were in a bind." Art glanced at his wife and she nodded. "That's when we came up with the idea for a competition. The contest removed the responsibility of choosing between two deserving families from us."

Butler pushed back in his chair. "However, Ryan came up

with a deal that will help us all out, especially with the new developments with the Colonel."

Grace patted Ava's hand. "I volunteer at my church. Anyway, I've been helping Lana and after what happened a few nights ago—" She placed a palm to her chest. "Well, as a Marine wife I'm sure you know how hard it is. We can't let a man lose his family over a lease."

When Ava speared Ryan with widened eyes, a kill shot pierced his chest. He should've told her about Schmidt's marriage break-up. Hell, he should've told her a lot of things.

"His wife took his son and moved in with her sister," Gracie whispered. "We were going to talk to you to see if we could come up with an alternative. But then Ryan showed up this morning."

"Don't worry." Butler sipped his coffee. "We've made a deal that will work for everyone."

Although Ryan shook his head, hoping to catch Butler's eye, the old man kept talking.

"It's a good plan," Butler continued.

"I can't wait to tell Stella," Gracie said. "She's endured many sleepless nights during Ryan's deployments. With his retirement, she can rest easy."

"Art," Ryan said. "I'd like to talk—"

"Ryan's going to buy my building across from the Opera House." Butler nodded in Ryan's direction. "I know it doesn't look like much, but he's got big plans."

The urge to yell *incoming*, grab Ava, and jump the railing washed through Ryan. Crap, this was not the way to break the news to Ava. He'd screwed up. Hadn't been fast enough to seal the deal.

Ava pinned him with a long stare, forehead wrinkled. Sweat moistened his upper lip and oozed along his hairline. If she'd sit tight, give him a chance to explain, she'd be excited— once she hung up the open sign for Robey's Rewards. If he groveled, she'd come around. She had to. They'd shared too much to lose it over a lease. Besides, he loved her and her chaotic family.

"I know you worked hard," Art was saying. "I wish I had better news, but I've added a bonus to your payment for the work. I think you'll be pleased."

Butler reached in his pocket and handed her a check. "You and your boys did a fine job. I showed the property yesterday and the prospect was very interested—even when I doubled the lease. And that's before you finished. As for your new location, Ryan can run over the plans with you."

"Plans." Ava's lips barely moved. "For *my* business?"

"It's not like we wanted you to lose," Butler hedged. "But Colonel Schmidt was in a bad way."

Like a slow-motion movie, Ava's complexion changed from translucent to fiery red.

"Ava," Ryan started. "I didn't want to get your hopes up in case I couldn't pull it off. My first deal fell through. But Butler and I came to terms on the condemned building. It's not perfect and I've had to adjust my plans—"

"We're talking about *your* plan for *my* business?"

Her pointed words rang in his ears like sniper fire. He'd expected anger and maybe disappointment. This quiet, dead-eyed version of Ava dried his mouth. Once they were alone, he'd layout the logic. Even a pissed-off businesswoman would understand the strategy.

He pushed to his socked feet and picked up his work boots from a mat. "Art, Miss Gracie, if you'll excuse us, we've got details to iron through. We'll get back with you about the property."

"It's too late for a private conversation," Ava said. "The College Street property has grown on us. It has more parking, which is necessary for loading and unloading furniture, and it's available right away. I'd like to lease it. But only if you keep the lease at the same rate as you first quoted."

When Butler rubbed at his balding head, the hairs on Ryan's forearms lifted.

"Well," Butler turned from Ava to his wife. "That price was set before the renovations."

"However," Gracie's drawl cut through her husband's voice like rifle fire. "Since you've done such an amazing job and want to lease it, we'll drop the price by..." Although her smile remained, her eyes narrowed on her husband.

"Twenty?" Butler raised his brows.

Gracie smiled. "Twenty-five percent."

Art's face reddened and he shot his wife a formidable frown, but didn't speak.

Ava hesitated, looking between Gracie and her husband, and then extended her hand to Gracie. "I need to discuss your offer with my family. If they agree, you have a new tenant."

"Excellent," Gracie said. "Go home and get some rest. Come by anytime tomorrow and we'll have the papers ready for you."

The interplay between Butler and his wife might have been amusing—if he and Ava were on good terms. At present, they weren't close to *any* terms. He followed Ava to the sidewalk, the rapid tread of her boots on the porch floorboards tightening the pinch in his neck step-by-step.

"Ava, let me explain." He hobbled beside her to the car.

Her soulful eyes narrowed in anger. "You made an offer for my business?"

"I couldn't let you lose your dream. You and the boys worked so hard."

"Me and my boys are a Marine family. We know the sacrifice." She straightened and lifted her chin. "The sad thing is I worried if my boys would accept you and if you could understand my sons. I never thought you didn't understand me. What's important to me."

"I know Robey's Rewards is important to you and your family." He was talking too fast. But if he slowed down, she might stop him. "I know you wanted to honor Josh. You've succeeded. He would be proud of his boys and you."

She hesitated. Ryan breathed. He still had a chance. She just needed a little time to get used to the idea.

"You're good with people," she said. "You manage the troops, my sons, Art, even me without a hitch. But I'm only interested in a partner." Her eyes moistened, and she blinked before capturing his gaze with determination. "You talk the talk, Ryan Murphy. I'll give you that. But in the clutch, you had no faith in me."

"I wanted to help."

She shook her head. "I lost my husband. But look what I have. My family dared to dream and we pulled together to make it a reality. We've healed. Kyle isn't angry anymore. Hope no longer clings to me. We've made a home in Sunberry."

"And Robey's Rewards?" he pressed.

"Will open in a few weeks."

"But not in the historical district." He held his breath. She could still change her mind, forgive him, and let him help her.

"In the building we renovated. The dream isn't lost because we moved the location."

Taking a chance, he stepped closer to her and touched a tear at the corner of her eye with his thumb.

Ava stepped back. "Do you know why we named our daughter Hope?"

What the heck did a child's name have to do with the present shitshow? But this wasn't the time for questions. From the sparks in her eyes, he needed to keep his mouth closed and his ears open.

"Why?"

"Because we were terrified. Raising three children on a Lance Corporal's pay wasn't easy. Three boys under ten. Holy smokes, it was Robey chaos. But we had hope. Hope for the future. Hope that we could raise the boys into strong men. Hope that our love could withstand another child to nurture and raise. That's what me and my children have—hope in our love for one another and for our future."

And from the distance in her gaze, his hope with her was fading. "I did it to help you."

She held up her palm. "I'm not a victim or a child, and I'm not looking for someone to take care of me and my family."

"A Marine serves. That's what I do. Service gives me purpose, helps compensate for what I've had to do for my country."

She tossed her bag to the passenger seat and turned to face him. "Is that what this is? Guilt over Josh?"

"At first." It was the wrong thing to say, but he couldn't lie.

"I was never looking for someone to hold me up," she whispered. "I was looking for someone to stand beside me."

She dipped her head and slipped behind the wheel. When he blocked her door from closing, her gaze met his. Tears misted her eyes, but the determination shining in their depths shot through him. It was over.

He swallowed, but it didn't soothe the burn scorching his chest. Marines didn't yield—not when everything he believed in, needed to survive was at stake. Motionless in the middle of the street, he fisted his hands at his side while the Explorer turned out of sight.

CHAPTER TWENTY-TWO

Men! She'd had her fill of them.

Ava climbed into the hayloft in her grandfather's barn and plopped down at the large opening used a decade ago to fill hay bales. With her feet dangling above the ground and the slope of her land and the pond stretching before her, the rapid beat of her heart slowed. Her thinking place always affected her that way. And mercy did she need to think.

"I take it we lost."

Ava pressed her palm to her chest. "Kyle, you scared the bejesus out of me."

Still in his dirty work clothes, Kyle stepped from the shadows and settled beside her. "It's a good place to get away from my siblings."

"Is Nate asleep?"

"He crashed five minutes after eating a mixing bowl of cereal."

"The largest bowl?" Why ask? Her youngest son's eating habits were legendary.

Kyle nodded. "We're out of cereal."

Ava leaned her head against the wood frame. The odor of

musty hay blended with a chilly breeze. Soon, the erratic fall weather would transition into a wet winter.

"So, let's hear it," Kyle said.

Ava huffed out a breath and reported the morning's events, except for her conversation with Ryan. She dug out Butler's check and handed it to Kyle.

He whistled. "Cool. That's almost double the proposal."

"It would've been useful for our opening—except we lost."

Kyle flicked a piece of hay and it floated to the ground. "That sucks. For Ryan too."

What did that mean? They'd lost the lease and she was in no mood to discuss her disappointing love life with her son. She hadn't been looking for love. Didn't have time or even the energy for it. She certainly didn't need another heartbreak.

"I used to think Dad was the baddest guy around. He could do anything." Kyle shot another hay missile to the ground. "But you've got him beat."

She turned to her boy. Even sitting, she had to tilt her chin upward to study his profile.

"You'll figure it out," he continued before she could respond. "And whatever you come up with, we'll pull together and get it done." He pushed to his feet. "Just thought you should know that."

"Kyle—"

"It's been a long night." He stepped away from her outstretched hand. "I'm going to bed now."

Although she longed to hold him to her chest, pretend her firstborn hadn't turned into a young man, she let him go. His independent streak came from her. Sometimes that was a good thing and sometimes it wasn't. Right now, Kyle was looking pretty good. She...? Well, she was tracking along the marginal path.

Although her heart hurt, she wasn't going to crawl in a

hole. She'd suffered situational depression after she'd lost her husband. She'd worked through it. And she'd lived in fear of a recurrence since that day. Fear had leeched away happiness, fulfillment, life.

The problem wasn't with her lover, her family, or a lease. It was with her, and she was ready to move forward—after sleeping for a week.

THAT EVENING AVA warmed the two rotisserie chickens and vegetables Michelle had dropped off with Whit. Hope was spending the night at the Frost home to give her family time to regroup. The aroma of seasoned poultry awakened her boys and brought them stumbling to the table. Although smudges circled below their eyes, they'd bounced back from the overnight of work. She hoped they'd show the same resilience for her talk.

Even though she suspected Kyle had already reported the contest results to them, she ran through an explanation.

Whit settled on the bench. "So we lost?"

"By ten minutes." She held out her hand for his plate. "Put it in perspective. We lost the competition, not Robey's Rewards."

Someone muttered something she couldn't understand, probably Kyle. She served equal portions to her sons and then served herself. On a normal night, forks scraped glass the minute she'd served herself. Tonight, silence blanketed the dinner table. She sipped her chamomile tea.

"Ten stinking minutes." Whit studied his dinner, but didn't lift his fork. "We were so close."

"We're going to be alright." *Better than alright*. She held out her hands toward her sons. Whit took hers and then elbowed Nate to put his fork down. Kyle completed the circle taking one of her hands and one of Nate's.

"We have one another. Not every family is so lucky."

"Major shouldn't have beat us like that," Kyle said. "He knew it too. That's why he complimented us—to ease his conscience."

She released their hands. "I know at least one of you is starving. Eat."

The scrapes and smacks brought a smile to her lips. Although not musical, the dinner cacophony meant healthy appetites and healthy sons. The competition served as a little bump in the Robey road to fulfillment.

"Are you aware of the problems in the Schmidt family?" She cut her chicken.

"Other than Derrick tries to bully us?" Nate said.

"The reason for his behavior." Ava lowered her tone to force her sons to listen to her words.

No one spoke.

"Colonel Schmidt recently returned home from deployment. He suffered from severe burns and PTSD."

Still nothing, but Kyle and Whit had stopped eating.

"Do you remember the last time your dad came home?"

The younger boys shrugged, but Kyle burned her face with a hard stare. He'd been older when Josh deployed and noticed more than his younger brothers.

"He was weird," Kyle added, his voice soft.

"He scared me," Nate admitted.

"Scared you?" Whit elbowed his brother. "He was our dad and never even spanked us."

Her sons had noticed more than she'd imagined. She sipped the tea, letting the warm liquid soothe her.

"Your father didn't frighten me," she said. "But I was afraid of the changes in him. He was a different man. War can do that to people. They see things that change them. That happened to Colonel Schmidt. Derrick might be scared too. Maybe he tries to be a tough guy to hide it."

"Picking a fight with us—" Whit spun a napkin on the hard surface. "We can handle it. He hurt Talley's feelings."

And another Ryan-the-protector in the making. "Talley is a strong young woman. She needs friends, not boys to protect her."

Nate bumped against Whit's shoulder. "Dude, you should know. She fights better than any of us."

Ava resisted the urge to pump her fist for the young girl. Maybe Talley's attitude would rub off on Hope. A girl needed all the positive role models she could find.

"So, what?" Kyle wiped his mouth. "You want us to be nice to Derrick or something?"

"Or something would work. More important, the Schmidt family plans to open a business, too."

"As competitors?"

Leave it to Kyle to get to the heart of the matter. "They're going to open a women's clothing store," she said.

Ava sliced a piece of chicken. The tender poultry exploded on her tongue. Twenty-four hours of hard work increased an appetite. Besides, her sons needed time to digest her information along with their dinner.

"The Schmidts have the same goal as we do," she said after three additional bites.

"Except they have our location," Kyle said.

"Working together brought us closer," Ava said.

Nate held out his plate. "Can I have more, please?"

"We weren't that broken," Kyle said, the old anger brightening his gaze.

"No, we weren't." She served Nate one third of the leftovers. "So the Schmidts have a harder job in front of them."

"What's that got to do with us?" Nate asked.

Ava explained Colonel Schmidt's injury and the reason Ryan had helped his fellow Marine.

Whit finished and pushed his plate aside. Kyle spun a

potato on his plate. Ava waited. Smart and compassionate, her sons would work through the issue. With time, they'd form an opinion, and then she'd present the decision before them—something Ryan had failed to do for her.

"So what now?" Kyle said.

"I was thinking." Ava took another bite and chewed. The blend of butter and garlic sizzled on her tongue.

Kyle strummed his fingers on the table. Whit waited and Nate finished his second helping. She chased the food with a sip of tea.

"We open Robey's Rewards before the holiday season," Ava finished.

Kyle squinted at her. "Like at the Columbia site?"

The boys exchanged glances while she savored her meal. Tonight, she was going to enjoy a hot soak in the tub and relax, maybe finish her book, or watch mindless TV. Three minutes later, she finished the final bite and rubbed her hands together.

"I missed the payback on the work we've done," Whit said in his halting style." It sucked that everything we did benefits somebody else."

"Main Street has no parking," Kyle said. "Moving heavy furniture in the building would be miserable."

"If we lease the Columbia site, can we move in...like tomorrow?" Whit asked.

"You have school tomorrow," Ava said. "But that's one benefit. We can move in as soon as we sign the lease."

"It's cheaper," Kyle said. "And with our bonus, we'll have extra startup cash."

"There's been a price change," Ava said. "Mr. Butler reduced the price by twenty-five percent." Actually Mrs. Butler had done that, but no sense in muddying the water.

"It's closer to Gina's restaurant," Nate said.

"Of course." Kyle thumped his forehead with his palm. "The food connection."

"We crushed the tile installation," Whit said.

"Anything else?" Ava stood and rinsed her cup and plate.

"Sign the lease," Kyle said.

Nods would've pleased her. She wasn't prepared for smiles.

"Done," she said.

"Where are you going?" Whit asked.

"Bubble bath."

Her boys didn't move. They also didn't blink. Something was up. Her crew could sniff out change like Toby sniffed out varmints.

Ava rubbed her forehead. "Let's hear it."

"You dumped the Major," Kyle said.

Whit scowled. "Why? What did he do?"

"Made her mad," Nate guessed. "He ate too much anyway."

Ava returned to her seat. The last thing she wanted to do was review the morning's events, but she needed to practice what she preached. Ryan had not only wormed into her heart, he'd made an impact on her children. They deserved an explanation. She started to switch on the burner for more hot water, then filled a glass with milk.

After a long drink to ease her scratchy throat, she gave them the down-and-dirty on Ryan's behavior. The refrigerator hummed. Toby walked around the table, his toenails clicking on the hard floor. She tapped her finger against her glass, and then wiped at something sticky on the table. Surely, her sons understood her position. It was obvious. Ryan wasn't a good match and she'd ended the relationship in a rational adult manner.

"So that's it?" Whit questioned. "He was trying to make you happy?"

Her boys might be growing, but that didn't mean she was going to share everything with them. They'd work out the idea that a couple was a partnership because she planned to demonstrate it to them—just not with Ryan.

"He's a pretty good guy," Kyle admitted in a begrudging tone. "He treats you right even if he does screw up."

"He's fun to be around," Whit said. "He treats us like... like we're smart."

"Of course, we're smart," Kyle said.

"Yeah, but lots of adults treat kids like they're stupid. Major listens to us."

Kyle shrugged. "I was getting sort of used to him being around. Hope loves him."

With his brow furrowed, Whit pinned her with a serious look. "Mom, you need to fix this."

She had fixed it the only way she knew how. By standing on her own two feet.

CHAPTER TWENTY-THREE

A Marine had to take a chance—even if it was the last one.

Ryan mashed the brake so hard the tires skidded to a stop on the skimpy gravel in Ava's drive. Parked a few feet in front of him, Ava's rattletrap car Goldie picked up the last rays of daylight. His lips twitched. Only Ava would elevate an inanimate near-useless object to something funny. Like him?

The crazy thoughts circling his brain froze his sorry butt to the bucket seat. His hand migrated halfway toward the lump in his breast pocket for the final time. He stopped. The memory stone wasn't his. For that matter, it had never been his, the same as Ava and the kids had never been his. He wasn't part of the Robey unit.

The words cut deep. But maybe... He rubbed his sweaty palms and squared his shoulders for a battle.

The sounds of the boys' voices and running water filtered through the front screen. He'd planned to arrive right after dinner. With the boys at clean-up duty, Ava would be free to talk—if she'd give him that much. Sweat oozed along his sides.

He squeezed his eyes closed and drew in a steadying breath. They'd had a week to get over the relationship bomb. She had to listen to reason, at least give him a condemned man's chance. When he opened his eyes, she was staring at him through the screen door. Based on the way her brows cut a hard slash across her forehead, his hope for a resolution fizzled, farted, and crawled into the dark corners of his mind. He'd have to wing it.

"I need five minutes...please." He'd grovel if necessary. When her eyes narrowed, he raised his palm. "I've got something for Hope." And her—if she'd ever soften her brow.

"It's from Josh." He cringed. His voice sounded like Goldie's car hinge.

He should've opened with different words, said something to erase the concern creasing her face. She didn't need additional angst. But it was too late for a retreat. A breeze tainted with a hint of rain evaporated the beads of sweat moistening his temples.

"I'm not here to discuss your business. This is personal."

When she opened the screen and joined him on the porch, a constrained breath eased from his lungs. Step one. But based on her rigid profile at the far end of the swing, he had a long way to go.

The scent of soap and something flowery tickled his senses, tempted him to touch. He remained alert, silent for a beat. At least she hadn't slammed the door in his face. But that didn't mean he was in the clear.

Ease into the situation. Check the perimeter. Listen, Learn.

But he couldn't stop looking. He'd missed her. Missed her old coveralls. Missed her hair pulled back in that Marine bandana. His finger twitched to push the dark hair from her face, run his palm along the smooth skin of her cheek.

"Tick tock." Her voice might be shaky, but it was hard as Humvee armor.

"Um, yeah. Robey gave me something right before they lifted me out. It was the night I took a bullet. I guess I was pretty bad. Robey put it in my hand and told me to hold onto it. No matter what happened. I shouldn't let it go."

Ryan swiped at the sweat tickling his temple. "I guess his order got me through. Anyway, they patched me up. I was due to return to my unit until Mom was diagnosed."

Nothing. He waited, but he didn't risk a sideways glance. Not yet.

"I didn't understand." He slowed his breaths. "It took me a while to figure it out—even after your memory night and the boys' stones."

He was making a mess out of the explanation, but the pressure in his chest might stop his heart. He pulled the rock from his pocket and held it in his palm toward her.

"He was working on it for Hope. Then I took a round and he gave it to me. I guess he didn't have time to start another one before...before he died." Ryan massaged his brow, but the ache in his head continued to pound. "I don't know why it didn't occur to me earlier or why it finally did.... Anyway, I wanted it to be right. You know, do it the way Josh might've done it if he'd had time."

Although the swing remained motionless, she was twisting her hands, knuckles white. She stared at his palm like he'd showed her something nasty and couldn't decide if she should shoot it or bury it. Wouldn't matter. He might as well be planted with Josh—after he saw that Hope received the stone.

"I didn't mean to take so long. But I didn't know how to engrave." He rubbed the stone on his pants to remove a smudge. "I had to special order the tool and then I must've practiced on twenty-five rocks until I got the H right. There're tons of fonts. I sucked at the fancy ones. But this one looks pretty good."

When he held it out to her the second time, she stared at him before opening her hand. Her small, strong fingers were shaking as much as his. He held on for a minute with the crazy idea he should hold on to her the same as he had with the stone. Hurt shadowed her gaze. He'd caused it. She closed her fingers around the stone.

He released a steadying breath. At least she'd let him do the right thing. His screw-up shouldn't impact Hope.

"I was going to bring it over last week, but I saw a stone in one of the giftshops along Main Street." He squeezed his eyes closed. Man, he shouldn't have mentioned the street. He waited. After a few moments, he figured he'd missed another Ava landmine.

"It was smooth and shiny—like glass. So, I asked the clerk about the polishing process." He'd been full of himself that day, casing the condemned building, dreaming of fancy shops and two-level garages. That's when he'd found the shop tucked on a side street.

"There's a special tool for that too." *Come on, Ava. Say something.* "Anyway, I wanted to give it to her—*if* it's okay with you."

When her chin trembled like she might cry, his throat tightened. The stone was supposed to make her happy, not sad.

"Thank you," she whispered.

"I'll need to embellish the story." Embellish, nothing. He needed to shut up. "I don't want her to think I've had it and didn't give it to her."

"The important thing is she'll have it now."

He didn't deserve a reprieve, but he'd do anything for a second chance.

"So, it's okay? It won't upset your family?" He squeezed his eyes closed. He never ran his mouth. He'd been trained to lead men and training increased his confidence, kept him on his game—until now.

Ava touched the stone with her index finger. "It's perfect."

Perfect? He huffed out a breath. He'd gotten something right with her—for now. "When the time is right, give it to her."

"Absolutely not!" She grabbed his hand and slapped the stone in his palm. "Josh gave you the job."

"Ava—" His head started shaking. He couldn't do it. Ava's tears were bad enough. Hope? Dude, she was a little kid. A happy kid who laughed with pony rides.

"I'd rather take another bullet than make her cry," he said.

She touched his cheek. "You're a good man."

Gentle, calloused fingers sent a shiver to his bones. No doubt that's why the dog wiggled when she rubbed its ears. Her lip lifted, not much but a little, in a half-smile.

"Hope won't cry," she said. "Your gift will make her feel included, special like her brothers. She won't think about the time she didn't have it."

But he'd always think about the time he didn't have Ava.

"I want to make her smile. When her tongue pokes through the gap from her missing tooth...I don't know...I feel... good inside." Engraving a stupid rock didn't make up for what he'd done. No matter how much he'd polished, it wasn't enough. Neither was he. But he couldn't stop his mouth when she stood there without talking. "You know when you sweet talk the dog and he wiggles all over? That's me around your daughter." No, that was him with her.

When she grinned, his heart thudded so loud she could probably hear it.

"That's why you should give the stone to her," she said.

He stopped his head from the bobbing thing.

"Okay, then." If that's what it took to make Ava happy,

he'd combat crawl through it—as soon as his feet received orders from his brain.

"When..." His voice cracked. He cleared his throat. "When's a good time to give it to her?"

"No time like the present."

Ava's tone sounded neutral. Which didn't help him a lick. If the woman would give him a clue. Crap, help a guy out. Especially a man groveling for his life.

"After I talk to Hope...Could—" Nothing came out. First, the Marine talks too much and then he's speechless. Action he could handle. His life and the lives of others depended on quick thinking and action. But words? Especially when the words meant the difference between Ava and a family and loneliness.

He swallowed. At least she was talking to him. Maybe in a few days or another week he'd come back, talk to her, help her understand. If he could make it that long. Finishing the rock and working with Schmidt had occupied his time for the past week. But Schmidt and his wife were back together, and the Marine was attending counseling. After he gave Hope the rock, he'd have his job in the Marines, but it wasn't enough. Not anymore. He took a steadying breath. One step at a time.

Ava led him to a pup-tent sized bedroom. In the corner Hope colored on a pint-sized table. Chill bumps pimpled his arms. Despite the yard-wide yellow streak inching up his spine, he forced his feet to move in front of Ava's soft footfalls.

"Hope," Ava said. "Mr. Ryan has something for you."

The cramp in Ryan's neck eased a bit. Ava's tone had softened and sounded almost encouraging. Hope's features lit up like a flare in the night.

Ryan blinked. The girl looked more and more like her mother every time he saw her—right down to the rounded shape of her eyes. And her nose. It was like a button. Amazing features came in that size.

He rubbed at the poke in his side and blinked. *The rock, Jarhead.*

What should he say? Sweat beaded at his temples and oozed along his hairline. With her dark eyes full of solemn interest, Hope cocked her head and a curl fell in her eyes—like her mother's. What if he hadn't been shot, hadn't come home to care for Mom? What if he'd saved Robey? He dropped to one knee and opened his palm. His hand trembled.

"Is that for me?" Hope touched the stone with a tiny, paint-crusted finger.

"Do you remember your daddy saved me?" His voice wobbled, but Hope didn't seem to notice.

She nodded. "You told us at Daddy's Memory Night."

"That's right." He swallowed hard. "Your daddy wanted me to give this to you." He transferred the stone to her palm. "He knew your mommy would take good care of you. But he wanted you to have this. When you touch it, you'll know he's nearby even when you can't see him."

"Daddy didn't forget me," she whispered.

His knees shook and his lungs burned. But he didn't breathe, didn't move, didn't want to say or do anything to spoil Hope's moment.

"See," she shouted holding up her rock. "Daddy made one for me too."

Air rushed from Ryan's lungs and he turned to Ava. Behind her, stood Whit, Kyle, and Nate. They were nodding and smiling, even Kyle.

When Ryan stood, the room shifted. Ava wound her arm through his and strength straightened his posture.

"I'll never be able to thank you for doing this," she whispered.

He had some ideas. Maybe start by whisking her off to a private place, just the two of them. Hold her, drink in her scent, listen to the lilt of her voice, talk about crazy dreams to build a treehouse for Hope, and teach her brothers the lessons he'd learned from his father. Once he'd proven to Ava how good they were together—because they would be totally awesome. No doubt about that—if she could forgive him.

The weight pressing on his shoulders shifted and he straightened. He couldn't predict Ava. But he had control of his actions. And he'd run through fire to earn her forgiveness.

CHAPTER TWENTY-FOUR

AND HE SCORES! AVA BLINKED HARD AT THE FILM clouding her vision.

"Outside," she whispered near Ryan's ear.

She hadn't meant to bark orders. But his masculine scent, blended with the spice of his cologne, had fogged her brain. That's why she'd directed him to walk in front of her like a boy banned from a party. Yeah, it was a little mean, but pay back could be a bitch—even for hard-headed Marines. Besides, he could worry about her decision for a few more minutes. When the time was right, she'd erase those lines wrinkling his forehead in a big way.

When she motioned toward the pond, a flicker of hope removed some of the beaten-puppy look clouding his handsome features. The crisp evening air straightened her spine and her resolve. Stars dotted the evening sky and the last remnants of daylight painted the horizon. She wound her arm through his, loving the strength of his corded forearm beneath her fingertips.

A doe at the edge of the pond looked up, her black nose quivering. Ryan halted.

"She comes every evening to drink," Ava whispered. "Last spring she had a fawn. It's probably grown now."

His muscles coiled and softened beneath her fingers, but he didn't speak. The exposed skin on her forearm pimpled. Hesitation was atypical for her Marine. Ryan embodied self-confidence, marching into a situation with authority. He'd made Hope's day. Still, the man exasperated her one minute and amazed her the next. She couldn't predict the outcome of the next few minutes, but it was time to let him speak his mind and discuss their definition of independence.

Although patience had never been her strong suit, she waited—and nearly chewed a hole in her bottom lip. After a moment, the doe walked to the woods, triggering another coil and release beneath her fingertips.

"You're right about partnerships." He huffed out a breath. "But wrong about my motivation. I was afraid you'd withdraw from the competition if you knew Schmidt had escalated. You'd give up your dream to help someone else."

"And you were protecting me from myself?" How could he annoy and touch her heart at the same time?

He reached out to her. "I was wrong. When a guy's spent his life learning to serve and protect, it's hard to change. But I'm working on it."

Good to know she wasn't the only work-in-progress around here.

"That's why—"

She jerked her hand from his and planted her fists on her hips. After all they'd been through, he had the nerve to make more plans for *her*. "Ryan Murphy, are you serious?"

His hands came up. "Hear me out. I'm throwing it out there for your approval."

"You've been *throwing* things out for the past few weeks."

"I'm not used to groveling."

Okay. Maybe, just maybe, her man was working out that

she wanted him planning *with* her not *for* her. Still, a gal kind of liked to see her special man grovel—just a little.

"Since you're going to need more time to paint scenes, I'll run Robey's Rewards."

"I'm not hiring and you already have a job you like."

He raised his ridiculous brows, twice. "I'd like working near you. You can paint in the back room and I'll run the front."

"Robey's Rewards is not the kind of shop where people break down the doors to get in. I'll have plenty of time to paint during the down time. Besides, I can't afford you."

"Will work for love."

A little snort escaped before she nipped her lip. "You work for Uncle Sam. I'll handle Robey's Rewards."

"That might be a problem."

Her spine went ramrod stiff. He wouldn't dare pull something else. Not after she'd put him on ice for over a week. "My tolerance for problems is nearing the limits."

"This is totally not my fault. Mom saw a picture of your clock tower chest and asked for a copy. I didn't think you'd mind." He grimaced. "I had no idea this would happen. And it's not like you've been open to opinions for the past few days." His face twisted into a wry smile. "At least not from me."

"News flash. You're still on my latrine list."

"Yes, ma'am. I got that loud and clear."

She was kind of getting into the commander role. "Carry on."

"I've had at least ten calls this week," he said. "Everyone is blown away by the clock tower painting. The operator of the Opera House wants you to paint an antique parson's table to display in the lobby. Lana Schmidt asked if you painted counters. Everyone wants to know how to contact you."

Ten calls? Was he exaggerating?

"I didn't give out your contact information." He dug a paper out of his front pocket. "But I've got a list of business owners and numbers."

The hum in her ears halted and a chilly breeze lifted her hair from her temples.

"Do you make coconut pie?" Ryan had an expectant look on his face.

"What does pastry have to do with my furniture scenes?"

"If you bake my friend Sonny a pie, he'll discount plaques for your work. You know, nice signs to place over your furniture in public places?" He lifted his hands. "Furniture scene created by Ava Robey, plus your contact information. It's a good idea. You probably need a website featuring your work, too."

Her dreams were becoming a reality. Not just the shop, but her art. She pressed her finger against his lips.

"I'm nervous," he said. "I figured if I didn't rush through my pitch, you might cut me off."

She tugged his shirt so he would bend toward her and brush her lips with his.

"I've missed that," he murmured.

"I've missed you—even if you're still looking for ways to run my life."

"Think you can keep me in line?"

Although she shook her head, her sappy smile gave her away.

He dug in the front of his jeans and held out another stone with an A and an R engraved on the surface. "It's kind of lame. But I like the memory stone idea. Maybe when you touch it, it will remind you I'm offering my hand. Not as a handout or a hand up. But as someone to stand by your side, shoulder to shoulder when life knocks us down."

"I think you know me better than I know myself." But she was learning too.

"You already own my heart." He folded his calloused hands over hers with the stone between them. "Just give me the nod and I'll retire."

"No," she whispered. "I mean, thank you. That's an amazing offer. But my love doesn't require you to sacrifice your dreams for mine. We have enough love to support two dreams."

He was shaking his head. "The Corps was the family I couldn't have. But I found my family— if you'll say yes."

His soft dark gaze prodded her heart. She moved her arm, but he held her hands captive in his with the stone between them—like their hearts.

"I had a missing piece too." She shook her head. "I needed a community. Sunberry is your home. You've helped make it mine."

She held her breath and waited. An owl hooted in the distance and a breeze ruffled his thick hair. When he smiled, the clouds parted for a full moon—free and light.

"So does that mean you'd consider partnering with another Marine?" he said.

There must be something wrong with her heart. It was pounding like it might beat a hole in her ribcage. Maybe she was suffering a heart attack or one of those murmur conditions. Which would totally suck, especially after she'd finally found the light.

"Did you buy that rundown building?"

"I retracted my offer," he said.

When he rubbed the back of his neck and looked away, she suppressed the urge to clap her hands over her ears. Not another stinking *but.* Instead, a huge belly laugh rolled out of her and echoed in the evening air.

Ryan picked her up and spun her around. "We'll make copies of that picture and post it all over town."

Her laughter stopped the croaks around the pond. She

loved this side of him, rushing his words, trying to please her. When he was unsure, her strength would support him like a true partner.

"Back up," she said.

"Yes, ma'am." He eased her feet to the ground. "Was it the photo or the pie?"

"Thank your mother for spreading the word. I appreciate her thoughtfulness. However—"

"Is this where you get mad?" he said.

"This is where we discuss your future. You retracted your offer and—"

He winked. "I couldn't make long-term plans without consulting my partner."

When her lip twitched, he shot her the cutest look with so much hope in his dark gaze—along with a promise.

"I'd be interested in your thoughts about long-term partnerships," she said.

"Yes, ma'am." He smiled. "Orders received and understood."

Her heart beat a happy dance until his smile faded. He studied the crease in his trousers.

"I want this so much." He cleared his throat. "I don't want to blow my chance. I can't imagine a life without you and your family"

"Partners watch out for one another." She wrapped her arms around his neck. "Raising four children comes with lots of land mines."

"Covered." He glanced at her mouth. "I'll probably make more mistakes. But if you give me a chance, I'll never quit trying to be what you want and need."

Air rushed from her lungs.

"Did we make it through the gauntlet?" he said.

She brushed her lips against his. "I think so—for now."

"Permission to kiss you, Ava Robey."

With his breath mingling with hers, words whirled in her head but nothing came out. She nodded. Heaven help her, she was drowning in him. Heart to heart, mouth to mouth, gasp for gasp. Her thoughts dimmed. A groan vibrated deep in his chest.

"You're killing me, woman," he whispered.

"No talking." She reclaimed his lips.

She couldn't breathe. Didn't want to. He pulled away.

"Don't stop," she whispered between quick kisses along the seam of his mouth.

His mouth bowed upward. Resigned, she rested her forehead against his chest, her ragged breaths breaking the silence.

"Just watching your back," he said. "Nate already gave me the stink-eye."

"Whit told me I better fix us," she said. "And Kyle confessed you were growing on him."

With every illuminated nerve ending screaming in protest, she peeled away from him. "However, that doesn't mean I want my sons to find their mother painted to your body like one of my scenes."

He grinned. "A kinky woman? Now, every time I smell paint I'll be in trouble."

She smoothed the front of his shirt when she wanted to tear it from his shoulders. "Stand down, Marine."

He held her close. His warmth seeped into her flesh and settled bone deep.

"Life sure has interesting twists." She turned toward the welcoming lights from Gran's house—her house now. "I came back to honor Josh and bond my family."

He squeezed her hand. "Mission accomplished."

"Not quite." She snuggled closer to his side. "You showed me the way home."

PLEASE LEAVE A REVIEW

If you have enjoyed this book, please leave me a review on, Goodreads, and your favorite retailer: Home to Stay.

Reviews help readers find books from people who have enjoyed a story and help me improve my craft. Yes, your opinion matters. If you can spare just five minutes to leave even a one or two line review, it would be so helpful in this book's success.

- To write a Goodreads review, go to Goodreads.com and type **Home to Stay** in the search field. Click on the title, scroll down and click on the Write a review button.

- For an Amazon review, select Kindle Books from the Amazon menu at the top of the page and type **Home to Stay** in the search field. Click on the title, scroll down the left side of the page, and click write a customer review button.

Thanks so much!

Becke

PLEASE STAY IN TOUCH!

Thank you for the opportunity to share my Sunberry world with you. I hope you enjoyed the Murphy family. If so, you'll want to read Whit's romance, Murphy's Secret available in print and ebook on Amazon. Also, stay tuned for **Murphy's Debt**, Kyle Murphy's romance coming in the summer of 2021.

If you enjoyed your visit to Sunberry and would like to know more about my CLOCKTOWER ROMANCES, you can connect with me in the following ways:

1. Leave me a review at your favorite retailer and GOODREADS and follow me.
2. Refer me to a friend.
3. Become a Book Mate and SIGN up for my TURNER TOWN Newsletter from my website. All subscribers are sent links to Becke's Book Mates, my private FB group.
4. Like my Facebook fan page, BECKE TURNER AUTHOR
5. Visit my website: www.Becketurner.com

6. Read my health tips blog on my website.

I love to hear from readers. If you subscribe, you will receive the following items:

- Monthly newsletter, Turner Town News, updates
- Book Mates, my private Facebook group, invitation
- Stories behind the stories that I only provide to subscribers
- Video clips
- Book sale alerts
- Cover reveals
- New releases
- Health tips
- Recipes
- More free stuff

If you subscribe, I will never share your information. I value your time and appreciate your interest in my work. If you find in the future you no longer want book notifications and free items, you may unsubscribe at any time. To join, click HERE, or go to www.becketurner.com and fill out the subscribe form.

Thank you for your support of my books. As a special thank you, I've added the recipe for Robey S'mores and an excerpt from my latest Clocktower Romance, THE PUPPY BARTER.

Thanks again for reading.

ROBEY'S S'MORES

If the *Home to Stay* dessert scene stimulated your mouth to water for s'mores, I've provided the Robey recipe. If the scene stimulated your mouth to water for other reasons, you're on your own.

Here's everything you'll need to create this tasty and inexpensive treat—without the worry of a fireplace or firepit.

Graham Crackers – S'mores are messy but breaking the crackers into squares makes the dessert easier to manage.

Chocolate - My family likes the dark chocolate. We buy the regular size chocolate bars stocked in the impulse aisle of the grocery store because the candy is already scored to break into small rectangles perfect for s'more creation.

Peanut Butter – The Robey secret sauce. What's not to like about chocolate and peanut butter? Spread the peanut butter as desired but be careful. The fat in the spread gets mouth-scalding hot. Allow your treat to cool after removing from the broiler.

Marshmallows – I use the large marshmallows and cut them into 2 coin-sized circles, perfect to cover the square without overpowering the other ingredients.

Sliced Almonds – The almonds add the extra pizzazz for this treat. However, crunchy peanut butter would also work.

Instructions for single serving:

1. Break cracker into two to create 2 sides of cracker sandwich.
2. Spread 2 sides with peanut butter.
3. Place two chocolate rectangles on one side.

4. Place half of one marshmallow on opposite side.
5. Sprinkle with almond slices over chocolate.
6. Place under broiler just long enough to brown marshmallow.
7. Remove from broiler.
8. Press sides together to create sandwich.
9. Enjoy.

BOOKS BY BECKE TURNER

The Clocktower Romances - Contemporary romances set in Sunberry, North Carolina.

HOME TO STAY

CAROLINA COWBOY

LOVING TROUBLE

MURPHY'S SECRET (Whit Murphy's romance)

THE PUPPY BARTER

MURPHY'S CINDERELLA (Kyle Murphy's romance)

To provide readers with discounted books, I've bundled Clocktower Romances in the following collections:

THE ClOCKTOWER ROMANCE COLLECTION, Books 1-3

- HOME TO STAY
- CAROLINA COWBOY
- MURPHY'S SECRET

THE MURPHY MEN COLLECTION, Books 1, 3, 5

- HOME TO STAY
- MURPHY'S SECRET
- MURPHY'S CINDERELLA

THE FEEL GOOD COLLECTION, Books 1, 4, 5 (coming in December 2021)

- HOME TO STAY
- THE PUPPY BARTER
- MURPHY'S CINDERELLA

WHAT OTHERS ARE SAYING

My FB followers may recall multiple posts about my writing awards. Stories change titles as often as women change shoes and Ava and Ryan's story was first titled *Murphy's Debt* and *Jamestown Homecoming* before my agent advised the current title *Home to Stay*.

Authors enter writing contests to test the story opening and to receive feedback on the pros. I consider it trial by fire because authors tend to be jaded readers and sometimes harsh critics. However, their criticism improves stories for readers. I've listed the awards presented to Home to Stay and a few lines of the comments I've received below:

Writing Awards

Golden Heart finalist
Maggie Winner
Golden Rose winner
Molly winner
Fabulous Five winner
Ignite the Flame winner
Beacon finalist
Catherine finalist
Linda Howard finalist
Fool for Love finalist
Pages from the Heart finalist

Comments on *Home to Stay*

1. This is a really well written story that held my interest throughout. Great characterization.

2. I really enjoyed this story. There is so much good in it and you've done a wonderful job with bringing it out. I love the characters, the boys, the single mom.
3. I especially like how you showed the different personalities of all the children, and how that reflected in their mother.
4. Great lines from each of the characters--and you've mastered teen boy grunt-speak!
5. This is a wonderful story with a great cast of characters.

ACKNOWLEDGMENTS

To use one of Dad's favorite euphemisms, writing fiction is *a hard nut to crack*. This story, along with the countless others I've created, was a labor of love. Without the support, information sharing, and advice of the following, this book would continue to reside in an external drive folder:

- The amazing women in Carolina Romance Writers (CRW) and Georgia Romance Writers (GRW) for sharing the highs and lows of my writing journey.
- My 2019 Golden Heart Award class, The Omegas, for sharing my best Cinderella conference and providing ongoing support.
- A critique partner extraordinaire and personal cheerleader, Peggy Anderson.
- My son for his military review and his continuous question, *when's that book coming out.*
- My daughter who had the wisdom and the courtesy not to ask.
- My son-in-law for providing duties at Camp Lejeune.

A special thanks to my husband, who persuaded me to attend my first writing conference, never complained about his Honey-Do List, and never questioned the time and resources required to follow this dream.

Home to Stay

Written by Becke Turner

Cover Design by Ebook Cover Designs

Edited by Margaret Anderson

This book is a work of fiction. Names, characters, places, and incidents either are products of the author's imagination or are used fictitiously. Any resemblance to actual persons, living or dead, events, or locales is entirely coincident.

Published by Special-T Publishing, LLC

ISBN - 978-1-953651-01-3

Library of Congress Control Number:

First Edition

First Printing --

Webpage: https://www.becketurner.com

Facebook: https://www.facebook.com/rebecca.turner.5891

Twitter: https://twitter.com/BeckeTurner

Amazon Author Page: https://www.amazon.com/Becke-Turner/e/B08N9RDR19

FB Author: https://www.facebook.com/Becke-Turner-Author-113219977250594

Goodreads Author Page: Goodreads.com/user/show/15034744

Book Mates: www.becketurner.com/?page_id=1076

Newsletter: TURNER TOWN

Health Blog: https://becketurner.com/category/blog

PAALS: https:https://www.paals.org

Made in the USA
Monee, IL
26 March 2022